...er
...e,
...ittle unsure of himself.

"Hi." She was breathless. She couldn't help it. She couldn't hide it from him. She never thought she would see him again, but he was at her doorstep.

"Hi. I know it's early, but I was hoping I could take you out for lunch today."

She grabbed his arm and tugged him inside without saying anything.

"I should have called. I was going to call, but I didn't have your number."

She smiled. He definitely seemed uncertain at the moment and it amused her. He was such a beautiful man with a smile that must have made hundreds of women jump out of their underwear. Yet he acted as if she might turn him down.

It was wildly satisfying to her. She stepped forward, looped her arms around his neck and kissed him lightly on the lips. "You want to take me out, huh?"

Dear Reader,

Have you ever had an overpowering connection with someone that you couldn't explain? In *Tempted at Twilight*, you'll meet Elias and Cricket, total opposites who can't understand why they just can't get enough of each other. I hope you enjoy reading about them as much as I enjoyed writing about them!

Happy reading!

*Jamie*

# Tempted AT Twilight

## Jamie Pope

**HARLEQUIN**® KIMANI™ ROMANCE

Recycling programs
for this product may
not exist in your area.

ISBN-13: 978-0-373-86518-5

Tempted at Twilight

For questions and comments about the quality of this book please contact us
at CustomerService@Harlequin.com.

**H HARLEQUIN®**
™ www.Harlequin.com

**Printed in U.S.A.**

**Jamie Pope** first fell in love with romance when her mother placed a novel in her hands at the age of thirteen. She became addicted to love stories and has been writing them ever since. When she's not writing her next book, you can find her shopping for shoes or binge watching shows on Netflix.

## Books by Jamie Pope

### Harlequin Kimani Romance

*Surrender at Sunset*
*Love and a Latte*
*A Vow of Seduction* with Nana Malone
*Kissed by Christmas*
*Mine at Midnight*
*Tempted at Twilight*

To every girl who wears her Blerd status proudly.

# Chapter 1

"Have you taken leave of your senses?"

Elias Bradley sat in the chief of surgery's office and quietly listened as she berated him. It wasn't the first time she had done so. He seemed to have a way of getting under his boss's skin.

"You're not even cleared to be back yet, and you get into an altercation with a patient's boyfriend?"

Elias's already injured hand was radiating with pain, a reminder of the scuffle he had gotten into, but he remained silent, knowing it was better not to speak until Dr. Lundy was done yelling.

"How can I make you head of trauma if you act so impulsively?"

*Impulsive.*

It wasn't the first time he had heard that word used to describe him. Teachers. Girlfriends. Even his own family had said it. But being impulsive wasn't always a bad thing. His rash decisions had gotten him pretty far.

"With all due respect, ma'am. One of the things that makes me a good trauma surgeon is the fact that I think and act very quickly. I saw a man grab a patient and try to yank her out of the hospital before she could be treated. I feel that my actions were necessary and in the end protected that patient from further harm."

He was impressed with how calmly he defended himself. He wanted to scream, *That guy was an abusive jackass. Somebody should have kicked his ass a long time ago.* But he kept that in. Sometimes he did think before he acted.

"You punched him!" she roared. "Hard enough to break his nose, and even if I cared about his face or the potential lawsuit that might be coming, it doesn't compare to how much I care about your hands. What good is a surgeon who cannot operate? Right now, you are a highly paid pain in my behind."

He had never heard the normally proper chief speak that way, but he had never seen her this enraged before, either. "I was only in the hospital to try to make myself useful. Even if I can't operate, I can work in the ER. I can still see patients."

"No, you cannot. I handpicked your orthopedic surgeon and your occupational therapist. They have both reported to me that you are nowhere near able to return to surgery, that even if you weren't a surgeon, that you would need to be on light duty. Working in the ER in the biggest, busiest hospital in Miami isn't anyone's idea of light duty. And taking into account your penchant for championing the abused and less fortunate, I'm afraid I'm going to have to ban you from the hospital until you are medically cleared."

"You're banning me!" He'd never thought it would have come to that. At most he'd thought she would yell at him and relegate him to paperwork, which he would be fine with, because he loved being in the hospital. He loved the sights and the smells and knowing that what he did made a difference. He didn't have much else in his life at the moment. His siblings were all very happily married and busy with their own families. There was no special woman to go home to. His life revolved around the hospital. He ate all his meals there. He slept there much of the time. Hell, all the people he socialized with worked there. He wasn't sure what he would do with himself if he couldn't come to work.

"Yes, you are banned. I have put an alert out to all the security guards that if they find you here, you are to be escorted out. Your swipe card has been de-activated."

"You're treating me like a criminal!"

"No, I'm treating you like an asset that needs to be protected." She took a calming breath. "You are probably one of the most talented young surgeons

I've seen in years, and you are excelling in a difficult, highly specialized field. You want to take over as head of trauma, but how can I promote you if I can't trust you to act rationally? Your hand is not even a quarter of the way healed, and you go and punch someone. Did you think about your career? Did you think about the potentially irrevocable damage you could have done to your future?"

The truth was he hadn't thought of it at all. He'd just acted. That big guy dragging that scared woman through the ER had made his blood boil. He wished he could say that if it happened again, he would have called security or ignored it, but he knew himself too well. Hand damage be damned. He still would've knocked that guy on his ass and given him a big taste of his own medicine.

He had two sisters. He hoped some guy would do the same for them if they were ever in that situation.

"You have nothing to say to that?"

"Nothing that wouldn't cause you to yell at me again."

She sighed and shook her head. "Go home, Dr. Bradley. In fact, leave Miami. You'll be out of commission for quite some time. Do something you wouldn't normally do. But considering the way you broke your hand, maybe you should sit in a room and not move for a couple of months."

*A couple of months.*

A nauseating twinge rolled in his stomach. He didn't think he could sit at home for a couple of *months*. He was immediately mad at himself again for breaking his hand. He had been doing one of those extreme mud runs with his brother and brother-in-law. He had crawled under barbed wire and had been submerged in a fifty-foot pool of mud. He had even run through fire, only to get tangled in the cargo net. He was on his way down when his foot got caught, and as he yanked it free, the runner just above him lost his balance and they both fell. The other guy had landed on top of Elias as he had put his hands out to break his fall. It was almost a twenty-foot drop.

He had replayed the incident in his mind a thousand times that day, but there was no way he could have prevented it. No way he could have changed the outcome. He had badly broken his hand and wrist, the pain so extreme he had passed out for a moment. He had to have surgery, from which he had yet to heal. His hand had already been swollen and practically immobile before he punched the guy. He was surprised he'd even been able to make a fist. Lord knew he couldn't do anything else with it. But that was the power of adrenaline.

His older brother, Carlos, was a baseball superstar who had been on the disabled list for nearly a year because of a ruptured Achilles tendon. Elias had lectured him about overdoing it, demanded that Carlos rest, acted like the smug doctor he was. But when he was doling out that advice, he'd never thought he would end up in nearly the same situation.

"Get out of my office, Dr. Bradley. You have been working nonstop since medical school. You're a young man. Take some time to enjoy yourself."

He stood up and left the hospital. It wasn't bad advice. He just didn't know how the hell he was going to do it.

Cricket Warren glanced at her phone…again. Only four minutes had passed since she'd last looked, but those four minutes seemed like a hundred years to her. She was seated in the bar area of a small oceanfront restaurant on Hideaway Island, waiting for a ghost from her past to appear. Well…maybe *ghost* wasn't the right word, but she wasn't sure what to call the person she was supposed to be meeting. They certainly weren't friends. They never had been. Just two people who happened to be born to parents who ran in the same social circle.

"Miss? Are you sure I can't get you something to drink?" the bartender asked her from behind the bar. "It's still happy hour for another fifteen minutes. Drinks are half-price. Our special is pineapple margaritas. They come in a pineapple cup. Everyone seems to like them."

Cricket was tempted. She wasn't much of a drinker, but she must look kind of sad sitting in a bar by herself, twiddling her thumbs. "Oh, I probably shouldn't. I'm still waiting for my friend."

"Your friend is late," a man said. He was sitting at the end of the bar with a domestic beer in his hand. His back had been to her most of the time she was there, his eyes glued to some sporting event on the large television over the bar, but she had definitely noticed him. She didn't have to see his face to know he was one of those hypermasculine men whose pheromones filled the air and made otherwise sensible women turn into a pool of senseless goopy jelly. His was broad backed, tall, muscular. He sat up very straight, which Cricket's mother would have appreciated. He wore his inky-black hair in overlong curls, which might have been considered boyish or feminine on another man, but worked on him. He was brown skinned, some beautiful shade that she couldn't begin to describe. And just when she decided that she had better stop cataloging his features, he turned to face her.

*Well...damn.*

He might be the most gorgeous man she had ever laid eyes on, and a tiny spark of recognition went off in her brain. She had seen this man before, but she couldn't immediately place where she would have met such an extraordinary-looking human.

Maybe in her dreams.

"Yes," she said quietly, hoping he wouldn't hear her embarrassing breathlessness. "My friend is quite late."

"Have a drink. They won't get mad at you. And if they do, they aren't the kind of friend you need."

She opened her mouth to speak but then hesitated.

"I'll buy you the drink. My sister-in-law loves those pineapple things. You should try it."

Cricket was twenty-nine years old. She spoke four

languages fluently and had studied with the best and brightest around the world, but she'd never had a stranger offer to buy her a drink in a bar.

Ever.

But then again, guys never made passes at pudgy girls with two PhDs who were named after bugs.

"Say yes," the man said to her, the corner of his mouth curling in an appealing way.

She swallowed hard and warned herself not to be the awkward person she was ninety-nine percent of the time. "I need to know who I'm saying yes to."

"Elias." He got off his stool and walked over to her, his hand extended.

"Cricket," she responded absently as she took note of his hand. Normally she introduced herself as Cree, because scientists named after bugs didn't usually garner respect, but this time she had forgotten and introduced herself by her given name.

He had recently had surgery. There was a barely healed incision running from his wrist all the way up the palm of his hand and one along his thumb.

"Do you inspect everyone's hand you shake so closely?" he asked. It was then she realized that she hadn't shaken his hand at all—she was holding it with both of hers as her thumb ran along the still-angry incision line.

"You shouldn't be shaking my hand. Yours is swollen. You should wave, or do that head-nod thingy that guys do."

"Would a wink suffice?" He took the chair next to her at the four-top.

"Oh, no. Winks can be kind of creepy, don't you think?"

He smiled at her, fully this time, showing off a set of perfectly white teeth. He became even more gorgeous, if that were possible. "They could be sexy, too. I guess it depends on who is doing the winking."

"And on the winkee. No?"

"I wouldn't find it creepy if you winked at me. Is your name really Cricket?"

"Yes. Like the bug," she admitted with a small sigh.

"That can't be true." He laughed. "Your parents must have thought it was a cute name for a girl."

"No, they thought I looked like a bug, so they named me Cricket. Cricket Moses Warren."

He slanted a brow at her. "Moses as in part-the-seas Moses?"

"I suppose, but I think I'm named for my great-great-grandfather, who was a conductor on the Underground Railroad. His name was Moses."

He winked at her. "It's nice to meet you, Cricket Moses. I am Elias James Bradley."

"Oh, how normal of you to be called Elias James. I suppose your parents were too unimaginative to name you after a noisy, beady-eyed bug and an ancestor of the opposite sex."

He grinned at her. "No, I'm named after a soap actor and my father." He raised his hand to signal the bartender. "A pineapple margarita for my new friend, and another beer for me."

"Friends now, are we? I don't even know one embarrassing thing about you, and you know two about me."

She wasn't normally so chatty with strangers, especially deliciously beautiful strange men, but she was feeling kind of nervous. "You know I just had surgery on my hand and I have very limited movement in it."

"Is that embarrassing?"

"Yes. I work with my hands. I can't do my job now because of it."

"You work with your hands, huh? Are you an MMA fighter?"

"No."

"A football player?"

"No."

"A boxer? Did you hit someone so hard your hand shattered in tiny little pieces?"

"I didn't break my hand at work."

"How did you break it? Freaky sex accident?"

"You're weird." He grinned.

"I know." She nodded, not believing she wasn't censoring herself like she normally would. "I have been my entire life."

"I like it." He looked down at his swollen hand and attempted to bend his fingers without much success. "I broke it doing a mud race. I fell from a twenty-foot landing and then had a 250-pound man land on top of me. My wrist snapped."

"Ouch." She gently took his large, swollen hand

in hers again and studied it. "Your hand should still be immobilized. Judging from the healing of this incision, you're about a month post-op."

He frowned at her. "Are you a doctor?"

"No," she lied—or half lied. She was a doctor, just not a medical one, and according to her mother, her PhDs were little more than expensive pieces of paper. "I just know a little about this."

"Who's this man you are meeting?" Elias asked as the bartender set down their drinks in front of them.

"I'm not meeting a man," she said as she studied the drink she'd allowed him to order for her. It actually came in a hollowed-out pineapple and was very interesting to look at.

"You're not?"

"No." She picked up her drink and took a sip. She found it delightful. "Why would you think I was meeting a man?"

"Because you are a beautiful woman sitting in a bar with a nervous look on your face."

"You think I'm beautiful?" She grabbed his beer and slid it away from him. "How many drinks have you had?"

She was smart. She was creative. She was great at board games, but she had never thought she was beautiful. She tried to look her best. But at most she was pleasant to look at.

"I didn't even have a sip of my second. I wouldn't tell you that you were beautiful unless I thought you were. I like your hair and your mouth and your huge doe eyes."

She tried to ignore the fact that his compliment made her feel warm all the way down to her toes. "That's why my parents named me Cricket. Because of my eyes. They call me Bug."

"Do you mind?"

"I didn't at first, but then everyone in school started to call me Bug, and not in the cute, endearing way my father intended."

He nodded. "That must have sucked."

"It did," she agreed. "I bet you were popular in school."

"What makes you say that?"

"I'm purely judging a book by its cover. You were a jock. You played football. All the girls loved you because you are so perfectly gorgeous." She swept her eyes over him again, enjoying how he looked more and more by the second. "You can hold a conversation, so I'm guessing you weren't just an athlete but participated in something like student council. You were prom and/or homecoming king. How much of that did I get right?"

"All of it," he said with a grin. "But you missed something."

"What?"

"I sang in the choir."

"That is surprising. Did you join to impress girls?"

"I liked to sing." He shrugged. "You never told me who you were meeting."

"A childhood…friend?"

"You don't sound too sure about that."

"I'm not sure I like her. I don't think she likes me, either. She always makes little digs at me. 'I'm seeing the most incredible man. I guess you haven't found anyone yet. I've been promoted at work again. Are you still doing research in that dark little lab of yours? Don't worry, you'll change careers when you get up the courage.' It makes me want to spill something on one of those thousand-dollar handbags she carries around."

"If you don't like her, then why do you see her?"

"I don't know," she said. "It's completely irrational, isn't it? But we grew up together. We attended the same private school. We took violin lessons together. We even have horses stabled at the same barn."

"Horses?"

"Yeah. My guy is old and overweight and his name is Seymour, and hers is this exquisite Arabian who wins prizes for his beauty."

"What's his name?"

"Adonis."

He shook his head. "Sounds pretentious."

"It is and he is! He's a mean horse. I bet he makes little catty remarks about the other horses behind their backs. My boy is sweet as pie. Beauty and speed aren't everything in a racehorse." She looked up at Elias, realizing that she was having a longer conversation with him than she'd had with any man that wasn't about science for the first time in years. And he actually seemed interested in what she had to say. Most of her conversations with the opposite sex were purely intellectual, about topics that most people without PhDs couldn't follow. And at times, they bored the heck out of her. Sometimes those men even asked her out, and rationally those men should have been stimulating to talk to. But this handsome stranger with a broken hand made her feel more comfortable than anyone else ever had. "Why are you letting me ramble on like this?"

"I don't know. We're the only two people in this bar. It seemed like we should meet."

Elias was being truthful when he told Cricket he didn't know why he was having this conversation with her. He had been feeling restless since he had been banned from the hospital. Staying in Miami, being around all the sights and smells, knowing that people were being gravely injured every minute, all over the city, and he could do nothing about it, was making him nearly jump from his skin. So he had escaped to Hideaway Island, home of his brother and twin sister. They had been supportive when he told them that he was going to be out of work for some time as he healed, both offering their homes for him to recuperate in, but he couldn't be around them, either.

They were both married. Carlos had a daughter. His twin was still a newlywed and so ridiculously in love with her husband it sometimes made Elias's stomach churn. They were all happy and settled, and Elias felt very out of place with them.

He was the only one of his siblings who was single. He didn't want to get married. In fact, he planned to remain single for years, but when he was with Carlos, he felt…unsettled. Like he was missing out on something. So he had escaped his sister's house and come to the nearby restaurant for a change of scenery.

He had immediately noticed Cricket when she walked into the bar. She was much different from the women he encountered in Miami who lived in slinky dresses with lots of exposed skin. They were overtly sexy.

Cricket was sexy, too. Oddly sexy, in a way that discomfited him. She was not his type at all, but when she walked into the bar that night, his senses went on high alert. He took in everything about her. She wore a short pretty sundress with a bold graphic floral print. Her legs were by no means long, but they were beautiful and thick—the kind of leg that a man liked to slide his hand up and down in bed. Her hair was in loose, almost fluffy curls. It wasn't a modern style. Hell, it wasn't classic or chic or anything, but it suited her. She looked perfectly sweet, with wide innocent eyes and beautiful full lips.

And he had been sitting with her for the past ten minutes, unable to pull himself away.

"Is there any particular reason you are meeting this woman you don't like here tonight?"

Cricket shrugged. "She asked to see me. It's been a while. Said we need to do some catching up. She's probably feeling a bit low about herself and would like to take a few jabs at me to boost her confidence."

"Why do you let her do that to you?"

"She must not be very confident if she has to tear me down to pull herself up. In an odd way, it makes me feel better. If someone that physically perfect has doubts about themselves, then I realize that I'm not so different."

"Everyone feels shitty about themselves sometimes."

"And that applies to you, too?"

"Of course." He nodded.

"Not about your looks. I wouldn't believe someone who looks like you would."

"Are you flirting with me?"

Her eyes widened in surprise. "Am I? I never tried before. I didn't think I knew how!"

He grinned at her again. He was doing that a lot tonight. He felt a little bit like an idiot, but it felt good. He needed any reason to feel good lately. Without the hospital he was feeling lost, empty. For the first time in his life he was idle, and he sure as hell didn't like it. "If you weren't flirting, what do you call it?"

"Being honest." She took a long sip of her drink. "Maybe it's this stuff that's making me extra honest this evening." They both heard the sound of heels clicking on the floor in the distance, and Elias knew that his conversation with this quirky woman was about to come to an end.

"I'll leave you to enjoy your friend. It was nice speaking to you, Cricket."

"I enjoyed speaking to you, too, Elias."

He got up and walked back to his spot at the bar just as a woman rounded the corner. Cricket was right.

Her friend was beautiful. She was tall, with caramel-colored skin and light eyes. Her body was toned, her hair long and ruthlessly straight, highlighted with different shades of blond. She was perfectly made-up and perfectly dressed. She was perfectly boring.

"Hey, Bug!" She smiled brightly. "It's great to see you."

"Hello, Giselle. How are you?"

"Great! Just great." She hugged Cricket. "What a cute little dress you're wearing. I could never pull it off, but you have never been afraid of wearing things you find in the thrift store."

"I didn't get this in a thrift store. I got this in a little boutique downtown. The one you're always talking about."

"Oh." She took the seat across from Cricket. "Do they carry your size there? I didn't think they carried anything over a size ten."

"They do," Cricket said, her nostrils flaring a bit.

"Good. You can carry the extra weight so much better than most people I know. I'm glad they have clothes for larger ladies."

Elias felt his nostrils flaring a bit. He wanted Cricket to tell the woman to go to hell.

"Everyone deserves nice clothing," Cricket responded cheerfully. "So what's going on with you? I know there must be something if you wanted to see me."

"I just wanted to catch up. You are one of my dearest friends."

"Were you working late? That promotion you got must be keeping you busy. You were nearly a half hour behind schedule. But I know you must have been too busy to text me. Us career girls have to really put our noses to the grindstone to prove we're just as good as the men, so I understand your tardiness."

Elias wanted to applaud Cricket. She wasn't a pushover. He liked that.

"I'm sorry about that. I was on a call." She reached across the table and gave Cricket's hand a light squeeze. "So, are you seeing anyone? I'm still with Arnold. It's getting serious! But don't worry, sweetie. You'll find someone someday. Women can have children well into their late forties nowadays."

That was it. Elias left his spot at the bar and walked back over to Cricket's table. He didn't spare a single look at her friend before he took Cricket's chin between his fingers and kissed her full, pouty mouth. He wasn't sure if that was the stupidest thing he had ever done or the best decision of his life, because he felt the immediate spark of sexual attraction in their kiss.

He lifted his head briefly, looked her in the eyes and kissed her again. This time she slid her hand up his jaw and kissed him back a little more deeply than he had kissed her.

"I'm sorry that took so long," he said to her as he slipped into the chair next to her. "I got our dinner reservations moved back another half hour."

"Dinner." Cricket nodded, giving him a conspiratorial grin. "Can't wait."

"Um," Giselle said. "Hello. I'm Giselle, and you are?"

"Elias." He nodded his head but didn't extend his hand to shake. "I'm Cricket's boyfriend."

"Isn't he gorgeous?" Cricket laughed.

Giselle looked stunned. "Uh... I... I—I didn't know you were seeing anyone."

"Well, Elias walked up to me and introduced himself, and I've been taken with him ever since."

"Oh, how sweet," she said, looking and sounding disbelieving. "I'm happy for you." Her eyes narrowed. "Tell me, Elias. What do you do for a living?"

"I'm a trauma surgeon."

"Here on the island?"

"There are very few traumas here. I work at Miami Mercy. I'm on leave right now. I broke my wrist and haven't been cleared to return yet."

"My boyfriend is in pharmaceutical sales. He's at your hospital a lot. Maybe you know him."

"I don't. I don't ever speak to drug reps unless they are bleeding out on my table."

"Where did you go to medical school?"

"Miller."

"You got into one of the best hospitals in the country." She nodded. "Did you meet Bug at a work function?"

"No. It was purely by chance, and I couldn't seem to get her off my mind ever since."

None of those things were lies. If it were any other day, he might not have been there. He might not have even given a second look to Cricket or cared that she was being disrespected by her rude friend. But it wasn't any other night. Tonight he wanted something to take his mind off not being able to work, and he was glad that Cricket was that something.

"So, are you getting serious? Your mother will be pleased, I'm sure," she said rather stiffly. "Who wouldn't love another doctor in the family?"

Another doctor? She'd told him she wasn't one, and he had believed her because he spent a lot of time around doctors and she seemed a little more free-spirited than most of them. But maybe he didn't know as much as he thought he did.

"It doesn't matter what my mother thinks. It only matters that I'm happy, and right this minute, I'm incredibly happy."

Giselle frowned, almost like she didn't understand what Cricket was saying. "I didn't mean to keep you two from your date night."

"You're not!" Cricket said. "Elias wanted to meet you."

"I've heard a lot about you." He nodded as he took Cricket's hand and raised it to his lips. "I want to know all of Cricket's friends."

"That's nice." She stood up. "I'm meeting Arnold tonight, so I have to run. It was good to meet you, Elias. Cricket, I'll call you?"

"Yes. Catching up with you is always fun."

She walked out then, and as soon as her heels clicked out of earshot, Cricket turned to him. "What on earth possessed you to do that?"

"I don't like the way she speaks to you."

"I can handle myself, you know."

"I know."

"You kissed me." She tilted her head and studied him.

"I did, and then you kissed me."

She had soft, plump lips. They were perfect for kissing. He could have just sat down beside her, held her hand and pretended like he was her boyfriend, but he'd kissed her. He *had* to kiss her. It seemed like the right thing to do in that moment. It might have been one of those impulsive moments that his boss was so fond of pointing out. There had been no thinking involved. His mouth just moved toward hers.

"Do you like tacos?" she asked.

He blinked at her for a moment, confused by the change in topic. "Yeah."

"What about frozen custard?"

"The soft-serve kind?"

"Of course."

"Yes."

"Let me wine and dine you," she said with a grin. "Or maybe I should say convenient food and converse with you."

"You are so weird," he said again, shaking his head. "I would love to have tacos and custard with you."

# Chapter 2

Hideaway Island was one of those small coastal islands that felt a little bit like paradise wrapped up in a warm blanket. Cricket had spent her childhood in Miami and her early adulthood in the New York area. But she had spent all her summers there on the island. It was how she recharged her always draining batteries, and tonight she felt full of electricity.

There was a beautiful man strolling down the beach beside her. His feet bare, his pants rolled up, his eyes taking in the scenery around them. She didn't blame him. Hideaway Island had to be one of the most beautiful places on earth. Especially at twilight, when the sky was purple and orange and the breeze kicked up and the air smelled like ocean and sweetness and something magical that she couldn't identify.

They had stopped at the food trucks lined up in front of the boardwalk and dined on a bench before they embarked on their stroll. She felt at ease with Elias when she shouldn't. He was a stranger. A stranger whom she had met in a bar! He could be some kind of con artist or murderer. She had already witnessed how smoothly he lied to Giselle about being her boyfriend and a surgeon at one of the best hospitals in the country, but despite all of that, despite all the rational thoughts that were always firing in her head, she liked him. She liked talking to him, being in his large presence. There was something safe about him.

There was also the fact that he'd kissed her tonight. She had been kissed before, but his had been the sweetest, because it had been so unexpected. She didn't have time to worry about her breath, or what he was thinking or how she looked. She had just let herself be kissed. And she had kissed him back. Tingles, warmth and sparks all felt like trite ways to describe how she had felt when he was kissing her, but there didn't seem to be other words for it. All she knew for sure was that she wanted to feel that sensation again, and it was going to have to be tonight.

Before her rational thoughts returned and she talked herself out of having more fun.

"Do you live on the island, or are you here just visiting?" she asked him.

"Visiting. I have family here. You and I met tonight because I needed to escape them."

"Not a wife and kids, I hope."

"Yeah, Serena is pregnant, too. I can't take all her complaining and the kids running around the house like a bunch of wild animals."

Cricket stopped in her tracks and looked up at him.

Elias took out his phone and snapped a picture of her.

"What the hell!"

"I had to get a picture of your face. It was priceless. You're gullible."

"You're a great liar. Let me see the picture."

"No." He slipped his phone back into his pocket. "You might delete it."

"Is it that bad?"

"No. It's cute." He wrapped his arm around her as they continued to walk. It was nice. His body was so large and hard, and for once in her life she felt petite and protected and liked for who she was. "No kids, wife or girlfriend. I'm single. My sister is a newlywed, and there is nothing worse in the world than being stuck hanging out with two people who are in love."

"I could think of a couple worse things."

Elias sighed. "I really like my sister's husband. He's exactly who I would have picked for her."

"But?"

"We're twins. We went to the same college. We

lived next door to each other until she sold her town house. She used to call me every day. We were close."

"You're not anymore?"

"We are, but it's different. Her husband comes first, which he should. But I kind of miss being the first person she tells all her stupid crap to. It used to annoy the hell out of me when she called me just to chat, but it was a part of my day. Now it feels like something is missing."

She smoothed her hand down his back, and he looked down at her with a sheepish grin.

"If you ever tell anyone I said that, I might be forced to kill you."

"Got it. Men break out in hives whenever they think someone might know they have a feeling."

"I'm a manly man," he said, deepening his already-deep voice. "I snapped my wrist and went in to work the next day with duct tape wrapped around it."

"You didn't."

"No. It hurt like hell. I'm pretty sure I started crying and passed out."

She laughed. "I don't believe that, either."

"I just remember my brother cursing and saying something about our mother flying to the States to kill him."

"Your mother doesn't live here?"

"Costa Rica. She moved there after my father passed away."

"Oh." She went quiet for a moment. "I'm sorry."

"Don't be. It's been many years now."

They continued to walk on in silence until they came up to a set of houses that were directly on the beach. "My house is right up there."

"Is it?" He looked at the house and then back at her. "It's nice."

"It is nice. Would you like to see it?" She was inviting him inside. She didn't want this night to end. It had been surreal and comfortable and wonderful, and it wasn't even 8:00 p.m. yet.

"Yes, I very much would."

Her heart beat faster as they walked quietly up the path that led to her beachfront home. She had never done this before. She had never met a man who she was this attracted to, who she wanted to spend so much time with. First dates had always been horrible for her. Awkward. Panic inducing. But she had met Elias by chance. There was no time for her to get worked up, to overthink, and tonight she wasn't allowing herself to think at all. She was living in the moment. Doing what made her feel good.

"Whoa," he said when she let them in.

Her home was beautiful, a gift from her parents, but Cricket really knew it had been her father's idea to give her this house when she finished her second doctorate. It was an overly generous present, but her father adored her and knew how much she loved this island and cherished the summers she had spent there as a child. It was nothing to him to give her this gift, even though her mother was against it.

Cricket, after all, was the heiress to one of the largest tech fortunes in the world.

"I know it's a little sparse right now. I haven't spent much time here until recently."

"Where were you?" he asked, looking around.

"My lab was based in Boston, but I traveled a great deal."

"I heard you say something about research. What kind of research do you do?"

She hesitated for a moment. There was nothing romantic or sexy about her job, but she was proud of her work. Her mother told her she should never be embarrassed of showing off her brain. But the older she got, the more she realized that men didn't necessarily want to date a woman with a bunch of fancy letters after her name. "I'm a medical scientist."

"A PhD?" he asked, stepping closer.

"Yes, I'm afraid I have two of them."

A devastatingly sexy smile crossed his lips. He then grabbed her bag and tossed it aside before he wrapped his arms around her and kissed her again. His lips were open, his mouth wet, his tongue warm. She immediately went slack, and he brought her body closer to his. Large, hard, hot. Those were the only words she could think of to describe him. He smelled so good, like ocean air and aftershave and soft-serve vanilla ice cream. She could get drunk off his scent.

"Tell me to go home," he said into her mouth. "Right now. Tell me to leave."

"I can't. You leaving is the very last thing I want."

"I was hoping you would say that." He pulled her cardigan off and kissed that little curve that connected her shoulder to her neck.

A moan escaped her as his hands slipped up her dress to skim the backs of her thighs. "You're so beautiful," he told her as he hooked his thumbs into her underwear and slid them down. "I want you so damn much."

She sought his mouth again, wrapping her arms around his neck and kissing him with a heat that she had never experienced before. She felt his erection against her belly, and it caused her to grow wetter, even more aroused than she was when he had started all of this. She'd had only one serious boyfriend, one sweet, lovely man whom she would have happily spent the rest of her life with, but he'd never made her feel this way. He never wanted her with as much hunger as Elias possessed.

"Take me to your bedroom."

She took his hand without thinking, and he winced.

"I'm sorry!"

"Don't be. You can kiss it better." He lightly pressed his lips to hers.

"When's the last time you took anything for your hand?"

"This morning. But I'm fine. Don't worry about me."

"I am worried. I need you to touch me all over my body, and for that to happen I need to know you're not in pain."

"If you take me to bed, I promise you the only kind of pain I'll be in is the good kind."

She smiled at him and took his other hand, leading him into her en suite bathroom. It was a luxurious bathroom by anyone's standards, with a huge jetted tub and a rainfall shower. There was a view of the ocean from the window.

"This bathroom is bigger than my bedroom," he said to her in a low voice. "I would like to spend some time in here if we can."

"We can." She went to her medicine cabinet and opened it up in search for a bottle of pain reliever. Some of the contents came spilling out, including her birth control.

"I guess I don't have to wonder about that," he said and then unzipped her dress. She had on the ugliest underwear. A beige strapless bra. Her white cotton panties had been left on the floor somewhere near her front door. She had never thought she would be here in a million years. She didn't even own sexy underwear, but Elias didn't seem to mind at all. He unhooked her bra and with his uninjured hand cupped her breast, squeezing it ever so slightly as his thumb stroked over her nipple.

She swallowed hard, almost forgetting what she was supposed to be doing. But then she remembered she wanted him to have two pain-free hands so that she could experience even more of his pleasure. She picked up the bottle and closed the door to the medicine cabinet only to come face-to-face with herself in the mirror. Only she didn't recognize herself. Her hair was windblown and wild, her mouth was slightly open, her lips pouty and kiss swollen. She was completely naked, and a large fully dressed man was looking at her with such open appreciation that it made her knees weak.

But the most marked change was the look in her eyes. There was arousal there, pure and naked lust. She hadn't thought it was possible to look like that. It didn't mesh with the image she had of herself in her mind.

"Do you see how sexy you are?" he asked as he pulled her nipple between his fingers. She bit her lip as the pleasure took over her. "I can't wait to be inside you. To feel you wrapped around me. I can't help but feel that you are what I need right now."

She trembled. The power of his words alone made her tremble. She took a small step away from him and filled a glass with water and handed it to him.

"Pills now."

"Open the bottle for me."

She complied, but she did it as she walked back into her bedroom, feeling freer and more confident in her body than she had in all her twenty-nine years. "Sit down," she ordered. He did so with a sexy grin that she was growing to love more by the minute. "Take these." She handed him the pills and began to work at the small buttons on his shirt. She knew his body was in spectacular shape, because she felt every hard-muscled line when she was pressed against him.

But now she could see him in all his glory. Beautiful brown skin covering tight abs and a powerfully built chest.

"I like bossy women," he said and set his glass of water on the nightstand before he pulled her closer. "Have I mentioned how incredible your behind is?" He cupped it, his fingers digging into her flesh.

"No, but a lady always loves a compliment." She pulled off his shirt and then pushed him back on the bed. She unzipped his pants and gave him a silent signal to lift his hips. She was growing wetter and wetter with each piece of skin she had revealed. It was something special to have a gorgeous naked man in her bed, one who she knew wanted her, one who was so aroused that she was afraid he wasn't going to fit inside her.

He pulled her on top of him, their naked bodies colliding. He groaned as her breasts rubbed against him. "Beautiful girl…" His voice was husky and breathy. He ran his hand down the length of her back. "Everything you do turns me on. We need to slow this down before I embarrass myself."

"I promise you," she started but trailed off when his lips looked too kissable to pass up, "that you never have to be embarrassed with me."

He rolled over so that he was on top, his body pressing hers into the mattress. "I want to touch you." She felt his heavy erection between her legs. She had wanted to run her hands over it, her lips, feel the weight of him.

"I really want this to last." He kissed her slowly and so deeply that she felt like she was falling. "Talk to me. Tell me something about yourself."

"As a child I had a cat named Sophie. She was fat and orange and I loved her to pieces. Your turn."

"My older brother played baseball his entire life, but I find the sport kind of boring and have only watched the games that he played in." He kissed behind her ear and ran his hand over her hip. "That was a deep, dark secret that you can never tell another soul."

"Juicy. Perfect for blackmailing."

"Tell me something else," he said as she felt him press against her opening, running his head down the length of her lips.

"Deep and dark?" she panted.

"The deeper the better."

She suddenly got overwhelmingly nervous. This had felt like a dream up until now, but he was in her bed, nearly inside her, and she had never thought this would happen. She had all but given up on men. "I have something big to tell you."

He must have heard the panic in her voice, because he stopped what he was doing and rolled them to their sides. "You're married. You share this house with your husband, and he's about to burst in here with a shotgun."

"No! Of course not."

"Boyfriend?"

"Strike two."

"You're not going to tell me you're a man." He

touched her between her legs, slipping a finger inside her to stroke her. "I can tell."

She cried out. "No. I'm a virgin."

"Excuse me?" She was lying to him. She had to be lying to him. Cricket was definitely an enigma. She was odd and brainy and probably leaps and bounds smarter than he was. But she was so damn funny and sweet, and she had the body of a video vixen hidden beneath her cute sundress and prim cardigan.

She was a sex goddess and he was lucky enough to be taken to her bed, and she was telling him that she had never been with a man before? He just didn't believe it.

"You don't kiss like a virgin."

"I'm only one in the technical sense."

"Explain."

"I was with a man for over five years who was born with a defect and couldn't…you know. It was fine, because sex wasn't terribly important to me, and he did other…intimate things to make up for it. But we broke up three years ago and I haven't made it this far with a man since."

"Have you tried? All you have to do is look at a man and he'll want you."

"I want you." She slid her hand up his cheek and kissed him softly.

He wanted her, too, and this revelation should have shaken him, but he was surprised to find that he wanted her even more. To be the first man inside her, to be the first man to have her body like this. "I'm glad you told me."

"You aren't going to walk away right now. It will kill me if you did."

"I'm not walking away. I can't, and I don't want to."

She let out a sigh of relief. He was surprised by her more and more each moment. She didn't see herself the way he saw her. Thick and delicious. So incredibly sexy that it made his teeth hurt. Being with her wasn't just a want, it was a need. For the first time since he had snapped his wrist, he wasn't feeling so damn empty. He stroked between her legs as he kissed her. She moved against his hand, her hips moving in a way that made it hard for him to believe that she was a virgin. He felt bad for her. She was clearly a sexual person with needs that had gone unfulfilled for so long. He felt even worse for that poor slob of a boyfriend. It must be torture to be this close to perfection without being able to have it.

He was going to have her tonight. Things had heated up so quickly between them. He liked to take his time with women. To seduce them. But he was too far gone. He had never wanted another woman so much. He was more than hungry for her. He felt like if he didn't have her, he would die.

Without giving it another thought, he slipped inside her. The noise that escaped him was primal. She was so wet and so hot and squeezing around him so tightly, putting him in extreme danger of coming before he even started.

He forced himself to hold back and not plunge inside her like he so desperately wanted. "Am I hurting you?" he asked through gritted teeth.

"Oh, God, no." She wrapped her legs around him even tighter, taking him deeper inside. "I need more."

He slid a little harder into her, which caused her to cry out his name. He kept his rhythm controlled and firm. He gave her deep kisses as he pumped away; he kneaded her flesh between his fingers, paid careful attention to her body, to what she liked. He kept his eyes open so that he could look down into her face. He wanted to remember this night, every single ounce of it, because he was sure he would never be able to have another night so damn perfect again.

"Elias..." She dug her nails into his back and squeezed around him so tightly that he lost all his control. She was trembling beneath him, her orgasm coming on hard and fast. He came with her, pushing into her one last time before he spilled himself inside her.

"Thank you for this, Elias," she said a few minutes later. "Thank you."

"Thank you for letting me be the man to do it." He kissed the side of her neck before he lifted his head to look down at her. She was flushed and glowing with perspiration and smiling. He had never seen a more beautiful woman in his life, and he didn't want to get out of bed to leave her. "Can I stay here with you tonight?"

"Yes. I would like that. There is nothing in the world that I would like more."

# Chapter 3

"You look chipper today," Ava, Elias's twin, said the next evening as they sat on the porch of the house she and her husband shared.

"Chipper?" He frowned at her. "I don't think I've ever heard that word used before."

"Well, it's how you look. You've been down since you haven't been working. I would say that I feel bad for you, but I like seeing you more often. When you're working I get the exhausted zombie version of you."

"Fourteen-hour surgeries will do that to you."

"Did you have fun last night? You met up with some friends?"

"Yeah," he lied, not knowing why he did. He told

Ava nearly everything, but he didn't want to share his night.

He hadn't just hooked up with some random girl. He took someone's virginity and spent the morning making love to her all over again. He *really* liked Cricket, but he wasn't sure if it was because he was in a weird headspace in that moment or if he just thought she was refreshing. If they had met in Miami, he probably wouldn't have spared her a second look, but they hadn't met in Miami, and this was no typical hookup.

He wanted to see her again, to be with her again. But this morning when he kissed her goodbye, he'd made no move to prolong their connection. He didn't ask for her phone number; he didn't suggest they meet up again. He had just walked away.

There hadn't been hope in her eyes, no expectation. She'd just thanked him and kissed him softly and waved him off. He respected that about her. He might have been weirded out if she wanted to turn this one-night stand into a relationship.

But she didn't seem to want to, and he wasn't looking for a relationship, either, but he wasn't sure he could just leave it at one night with her.

"I'm glad you went out. Are you planning to see them again?"

"I was just thinking about that myself. I might head over to Carlos's and stay with him for a few days."

"You getting sick of me already?"

"No…kind of. Yeah, actually. You and your husband kiss so much I wonder how your lips haven't fallen off. Though Carlos and Virginia aren't much better."

"They aren't." Ava smiled. "When you fall in love, really fall in love, you'll find yourself being the gross person you never thought you would be."

"I sincerely hope not."

"You can hope all you want, but when you're with the right person, you can't help it." She looked over to the house next door. "Since Derek opened up a new studio space, we can actually use our house as a house. This place is bigger and we aren't going to be using the one next door. We were planning to rent it out, but I would much rather have you there. You can come and go as you please, and you won't be subjected to my husband and me making out all over the furniture."

"It might be nice to go forty-five minutes without having to be subjected to that, but I don't want you to lose any rental income for me."

"Lose money? Ha! I was planning to charge you double market value."

"I might head back to Miami soon. I was thinking about taking a trip somewhere. Maybe I'll visit Mom."

"You'll last three days there. There are five women in that house. They'll smother you to death."

"They will," he said grimly. His mother and aunts were likely to kiss the skin off his face. But he had to go somewhere, because if he didn't, he would find himself going back to see the woman whom he hadn't been able to get off his mind all day.

Cricket sat at the desk in her office and stared at her blank computer screen. She was supposed to be writing. She had left her job to concentrate on writing her next book. She had doctorates in anthropology and biology, and she had just spent the last ten months in India and sub-Saharan Africa studying small pockets of isolated populations and the illnesses that affected them. She had notebooks full of notes, but today she couldn't make her fingers work with her brain. And it was probably because her head was still filled with Elias. Two days later and it all still felt like a dream to her, so incredibly magical that it had to be unreal.

She had been with Phillip for a long time. He had been incredibly sweet and gentle. He would hold her for hours and kiss her softly. But there was no hope of sex for them. She had been to doctors with him. They had seen the best in the world—no one could help them. She had assured him that it was fine. That the intimacy they shared was enough. And sometimes it was. He would touch her between her legs, using his fingers and his mouth to bring her pleasure. It had been satisfying for her, even though she felt something was missing. After a while they stopped being intimate altogether. He was more like a brother or a good friend, and still she'd been willing to marry him. He'd been the one to break it off. He'd said that she deserved passion and babies and a life he could never give her. She was deeply hurt by it, because she had never wanted kids and passion faded. She had never asked for a different kind of life.

But then she had been with Elias, who was gentle and sweet with her, too, but he was also strong and powerful, and she needed that. He had made love to her that night and once again in the morning. She had stayed in bed that entire day, in her used sheets, not wanting to get up and change them because she didn't want to lose the scent of him.

She kept thinking of how he felt inside her, that slow, hard slide that made her incoherent. Just thinking about him now was making her aroused. There was a persistent throb between her legs that wouldn't go away.

She knew he wasn't looking for a fling or a relationship, but she wanted to see him again, just to spend a few more hours in his strong presence. She simply liked him. She couldn't say that about any other man she had been in contact with for a long time.

Her cell phone rang, and she looked at the caller ID to see that her mother was calling.

Her mother, the brilliant Dr. Frances Lundy. Born into abject poverty in the projects of New York City, she'd gone on to earn a perfect score on her SATs and been accepted to all eight Ivy League schools. Frances had paid her way through medical school to become one of the top cardiothoracic surgeons in the world and the chief of surgery at one of the best hospitals in the country. And to top it all off, she had snagged herself a billionaire. Her mother was the most brilliant person she knew, and Cricket was still slightly afraid of her.

"Hello, Mom."

"How are you, honey? Your father is here. Say hello, Jerome"

"Hello, precious! I miss you. Come write your book here. We'll have so much fun."

They would. Her father was a giant goofball and the most creative person she knew. He'd invented a smartphone that could hold a charge for three days. It was the bestselling phone in history, and that was only in the last ten years. He had over 150 successful inventions to his name. Cricket often wondered how her parents got together when her mother was so by the book and her father was so off the rails. "I purposely didn't come home because I knew it would be too much fun with you. I wouldn't get any work done."

"And here I thought," her mother stated, "that you were avoiding the long interrogation I was going to give you about spending nearly a year in the most poverty-stricken, disease-ridden parts of the world. I worked incredibly hard to make sure you would never have to witness those conditions, and at every opportunity you go back into them."

"My research could help millions of people, Mom."

"I know," she said softly. "If you weren't so brilliant and kind, you would be a sore disappointment to me."

"Gee, thanks."

"We do want to see you. I'll be away at a conference for the next two weeks and then your father will be away, so we are calling to block off a date now."

This was common with her parents, having to schedule dinner a month in advance so they could all spend time together.

It would be a full six weeks before all their schedules aligned, and so they made a date to meet in Miami at her mother's favorite Creole restaurant. She was looking forward to seeing her parents in person. It had been a long time. She had video chatted with them three times a week while she was away, but it had been months since she had seen them last.

She heard the doorbell ring. She glanced at the clock. It wasn't yet 11:00 a.m., and she hadn't been expecting anyone. No one came to visit her on the island. Most of her friends were in academia and lived all around the world.

She opened the door, and her heart jumped. Flipped. Went right from her chest and into her throat. Elias was there, looking absolutely gorgeous and a little unsure of himself.

"Hi." She was breathless. She couldn't help it. She couldn't hide it from him. She'd never thought she would see him again, but he was at her doorstep.

"Hi. I know it's early, but I was hoping I could take you out for lunch today."

She grabbed his arm and tugged him inside without saying anything.

"I should have called. I was going to call, but I didn't have your number."

She smiled. He definitely seemed uncertain in the moment, and it amused her. He was such a beautiful man, with a smile that must have made hundreds of women jump out of their underwear. Yet he acted as if she might turn him down.

It was wildly satisfying to her. She stepped forward, looped her arms around his neck and kissed him lightly on the lips. "You want to take me out, huh?"

"Yes." He smoothed his hands down her back, which she found arousing and comforting. "Very much so."

"Why do you want to take me out? Is it because you want to go to bed with me again? I slept with you before. You have to know how much I enjoyed it." She kissed his jaw.

He shut his eyes. "I like you, Cricket… I just want you to know that I'm not just using you for sex. I took your virginity. That means something to me. It's a gift you can only give once, and I want you to look back on that night and not have any regrets about it."

Her stomach did a weird flippy thing, and she knew in that moment that she had tumbled a little bit in love with him. She cupped his face in her hands and kissed him with everything she had. "My room.

Right now." She slipped her hands up his shirt, feeling his warm muscled back.

"Lunch first." He made no move but kissed her again, his tongue sweeping into her mouth. "I specifically came here to take you out, not to sleep with you."

"It's too early for lunch…"

"We can have brunch instead," he said as he slid his hands down to her behind and cupped it.

"I look a mess right now." She kissed his neck. "I can't possibly leave the house looking like this."

"You look delicious to me."

"I'll need to take a bath. A very soapy, very warm bath. You want to join me?"

"I can't say no to you."

She led him into her bathroom and turned to face him, staring at him for a moment. She couldn't believe he was here. She had been thinking about him, craving his touch, and now he was here before her and that beautiful experience they'd had wouldn't just be a onetime thing that she would only relive in her dreams. But she was going to feel his hands all over her body again, and she almost couldn't stand it.

"What are you thinking about?"

"What are *you* thinking about?" she countered, unwilling to give up her thoughts.

"You."

"Good answer, sir."

"Take off your clothes. I've been thinking about seeing you naked for two days."

She stripped off her tank top and the soft cotton T-shirt bra that she wore beneath it. She didn't know how to be sexy. She had never felt sexy before, but being around Elias had changed her a little bit. She didn't feel like her normal academic self. She felt womanly and sexual and happy. "Your turn."

He peeled off his shirt, revealing his six-pack, and her mouth went dry. It should be illegal for one man to be so damn fine.

"Your turn again," he said to her in his husky voice.

She grinned at him and turned around to wiggle out of her shorts. She heard him groan in appreciation and took it a step further, bending over the side of the tub to turn on the water.

"What the hell are you doing to me?"

She heard his pants unzip and his shoes hit the floor with a thud.

"Don't move." She felt him behind her, and then his hands were on her hips, his erection brushing her backside. She instinctively pushed her behind toward him, and he slipped inside her. She was incredibly aroused. His slow slide inside her felt so incredibly good that she almost blacked out. He shifted their bodies so that her hands were braced on the side of the tub and she was bent over before him.

He pumped into her with fast short strokes that were different from the other two times they'd had sex. She was finding that she liked it, the frenzy of it. The sound of his heavy breathing, the sound of their skin slapping together and her name on his lips. Every hard push inside was bringing her closer to orgasm.

He chanted her name. Over and over again. He was enjoying her, enjoying being inside her body. She'd never thought she would have this feeling, but this man was an unexpected gift. Had he chosen to walk away this afternoon and never look back, she would still be happy. Because he had already given her so much in such a short amount of time.

"Please, Cricket. Please come for me. You feel too good. I can't hold on much longer."

He didn't have to ask, because she felt herself clenching around him, waves and waves of exquisite pleasure carrying her away. Elias let out a guttural moan and spilled himself inside her. After a few moments of recovery, he stood her up straight, pulled her into him and kissed her deeply. "I'm sorry," he whispered. "You provoked the hell out of me, but you're new to sex and I should have waited to make love to you in bed."

"Don't be sorry. I might be new to intercourse, but not to sexuality."

"That was the nerdiest thing I've ever heard a naked woman say," he said with a devastatingly delicious grin.

"I'm a nerd. I can't help it."

"You're the most beautiful nerd in the world."

"You're very good at making a woman feel appreciated." She gave him a quick kiss before she turned away to check the temperature of the bathwater and add bubbles. "I'd bet you end up going home with a lot of women you meet in bars."

"I don't." He shut off the water and stepped inside the large tub. He groaned in pleasure and then held out his hand for her to join him. She leaned against him and shut her eyes.

This was what heaven must feel like. The hot water. The scented bubbles. And Elias's large hard chest and arms surrounding her. "Why don't you take a lot of ladies home?"

"I don't date a lot because of my work."

"What do you do for a living? I don't think we discussed that."

"We did. I'm a trauma surgeon at Miami Mercy."

She stiffened. Miami Mercy? An uncomfortable feeling settled in the pit of her stomach. Her mother was chief of surgery there. She was his boss.

"What's the matter?" He trailed his fingers down her arm. "You don't like surgeons?"

"No, I love surgeons. I just thought you were lying to impress Giselle."

"I wasn't. I broke my wrist and am not allowed to work. My boss banned me from the hospital."

"Banned you?" The question came out more like a squeak. Her mother had mentioned him. She had been exasperated. Young, brilliant surgeon who was stupid enough to break his hand while participating in some foolish activity. Cricket knew it had to be a big deal, because her mother rarely spoke of her work. Elias must have infuriated her.

"Yes. I tried to go back and work in the ER two weeks post-op. I punched a guy I saw trying to drag his girlfriend from the hospital and hurt my hand again. My boss was so incredibly angry with me, I thought she was going to fire me."

Dr. Frances Lundy normally would have, but Elias must be that good. Cricket knew her mother wouldn't give him another chance if he screwed up again. She would fire him if she thought he was a major liability. And she was fairly sure her mother wouldn't like the idea of one of her doctors picking up her daughter in a bar. She wouldn't like it all.

Cricket absently picked up Elias's injured hand and kissed it. "You love your job, don't you?"

"I feel a little lost without it," he admitted to her and bent his head to kiss her shoulder. He loved the feel of her, the way their wet nude bodies fit together. He had been restless this morning after not being able to sleep at all last night. He had been thinking about her, in a way that he never thought about anyone.

Part of him knew it was because for the past fifteen years, he had been working with single-minded focus toward becoming a surgeon. Even before that, in high school, he had been studying, working extra hard to make sure his grades were good enough. And now he didn't have any of that. Not the smells of the hospital, not the thrill of saving someone's life. His days as a surgeon had always been unpredictable, but now his life was unpredictable with nothing-ness ahead of him. He had spent most of his days trying to figure out what to do with himself. But not now, not when he was with a sweet, beautiful woman who made him wonder why he had gone so long without one.

He hadn't planned on being there today. He'd told his brother and sister that he was planning to head back to Miami. But he had found himself at Cricket's front door instead.

"What compels one to become a surgeon? And don't tell me it's because you want to help people."

"My mother gets a kick out of telling people that I'm a surgeon. I like hearing people call me 'Doc-tor,' and I love cutting up stuff."

She looked back at him with a slight grin. "All very noble reasons."

"My father is the real reason I became a doctor. He once told me it was his dream to become a doctor. He was ready to go to college when his own father died and he had to take over supporting his family."

"He must have been so proud of you."

"He never got to see me graduate from medical school. He passed away when I was in college. A massive heart attack took him from us unexpect-edly."

He didn't know why he felt compelled to tell her this. He never talked about his father's death. His brother and sisters had each handled their father's passing differently. Elias chose never to talk about it. He had been the one with his father that day. The memory of his father's face twisted in agony would never leave him.

Cricket turned completely, looping her arms around his neck and pressing her chest to his. "I'm not going to say sorry again." She kissed him. "Those words never seem adequate enough."

"You're sweet," he told her. He felt like he had known her forever, but in reality she was a stranger he'd met three days ago. But he knew for sure that he liked her. Probably a little more than was healthy. "Turn back around."

"Why? You don't like looking me in the eye?"

"I do, but you've floated to the top and I can see your behind peeking out of the soapy water. It's incredibly distracting."

She smiled and pressed her lips to his. "I like being distracting. It's new for me."

"I have a hard time believing that. You are very sexy. Men must hit on you."

She turned around again, her back settling against his chest. "I spend a lot of time with brainy types like me, and I study how infectious diseases affect different populations for a living. I don't hang out at bars or nightclubs but once I tell a regular guy that I've seen a virus literally eat away at someone's brain, it usually turns them off."

"I would love to do brain surgery. I haven't gotten the opportunity yet. It's on my bucket list."

She let out a soft, almost musical laugh. "You are a very special man, Elias James."

"Thank you." She had a voluptuous figure and large firm breasts that he couldn't believe she managed to hide so well under her clothing. He touched them, running his fingers over them, enjoying the way her nipples went hard as he did.

He was aroused again. He was in a constant state of arousal when he was with her, but it was nice to touch her body for the sake of touching her. It wasn't going to lead to sex this time. That unexpected surge of lust had taken him over, made him snap and take her bent over the tub. He hadn't planned for that when he walked in here with her. He wanted to prolong it, to savor it, to turn her on so much that she was squirming with desire. But she was too sexy, and he couldn't go one second longer without being inside her.

"Tell me about this last boyfriend of yours."

"He was incredibly sweet, kind and gentle. He's a theoretical physicist and an even bigger blerd than I am."

"What's a blerd?"

"A black nerd."

He laughed. "I've never heard that term before."

"Of course you haven't. You are very far from one. You might be the opposite of one with all your muscles and raging testosterone."

"Hey! I like science and math. I'm a doctor."

"No, you're a surgeon, sweetie. They tend to think

that they are truly more gifted and talented than any other doctor, that they do all the hard work while other doctors simply diagnose. There's no nerd in you. You couldn't do what you do without some hefty confidence backing you up."

"You sound like you have something against surgeons."

"I don't!" She turned around to look at him with wide eyes. "I know a few, and most of them think what I do is a joke."

"What you do is important. I can remove a bullet from a heart, but I can't stop a disease from wiping out an entire population. Don't stereotype us all." He smoothed his hand over her stomach, unable to prevent himself from touching her.

"I'm sorry." She sighed. "I should know better."

He wondered who the surgeon was who'd showed her the nastier side of his profession. "Most of the things you said were true. You should hear how we talk about anesthesiologists."

She laughed again. He really liked her sweet laugh.

"You never finished telling me about your boyfriend."

"You want to know about my sexual history or lack thereof?"

"You like sex. You're very good at it. I'm just curious about how you could be with someone for so long who couldn't give you want you needed."

"I told myself that my love for him outweighed my physical needs. I loved his mind and our conversations. And he did touch me when I asked. He would research things that he could do to please me, and he would do them. But I knew those times weren't enjoyable for him. Even if he were physically able, I don't think he would have been that interested in sex. It's hard to face up to the fact that your partner would rather be reading than touching your naked body."

"But you stayed."

"He was the one to end it. He said we were living more like siblings than boyfriend and girlfriend. He was right, but I didn't think I would ever find someone as supportive and loving as he was."

*And now you have me,* he thought. It alarmed him. He didn't know why that thought had popped into his head. It was insane. He had just met her. So what if he couldn't get her off his mind? So what if she was the best sex he had ever had? "Relationships are hard," he said, more to himself than to her.

"I agree. I gave up on them after that."

"And love and sex and closeness."

They were quiet for a moment. He, too, had given up on love and closeness and sex. His quest to become head of his department had replaced his need for those luxuries. But human contact was important, feeling this close to someone was important.

"Tell me about your past loves," she said to him.

"There's nothing much to tell. My last serious relationship was when I was in medical school."

"What happened?"

"Residency. Hers was in San Bernardino. I stayed in Miami. I think she's married to a plastic surgeon now."

"Fancy."

"I know. Sometimes I wonder if I should have gone into plastic surgery as a specialty. The hours are better. The pay is ridiculous. I could actually buy a house like this and be able to spend time in it. Having a view of the ocean from your bathtub is something I could get used to."

"I thought you were going to say that you wonder what would have happened if you had married her instead."

"No. I liked her enough. But I didn't love her. I haven't thought about her in years."

"One hopes when they leave a relationship that they are forever burned into their partner's memory." She turned in his arms again and kissed him for a long time. "I guess this doesn't bode well for me. Our two-night stand will be a whisper of a memory to you."

"I won't forget you," he said truthfully. "I don't want to."

# Chapter 4

That night with Elias had turned into an entire week. One magical week of sex, deep conversations, breakfasts in bed and walks on the beach. They had only ventured out of her house a few times for food and fresh air, but when they did, Elias held Cricket's hand. Their fingers interlocked. It was the most romantic week of her life.

It was the sweetest week of her life.

But he had to go back to Miami, and she had to get on with her life.

She was being honored at a conference in England, and old friends had wanted to see her during her visit. She hadn't seen Elias in a month, and she found herself missing him every day. But the fact that he was her mother's employee never left her mind. She had grown up with a surgeon. She loved her mother, but her mother's career had always come first. She had worked long hours, and sometimes there were entire weeks where Cricket hadn't seen her. Her mother was determined to advance her career and not be seen as just the wife of a rich man. She was working her way to the top, and that meant there was less time for her daughter. As a result, Cricket grew to think of their housekeeper more as a mother than her own. She didn't begrudge her mother or her success. She was inordinately proud of all Frances had accomplished, but Cricket knew she couldn't fall in love with a man who was on the same path. Elias loved his job. He wanted to be head of trauma. He couldn't wait till he was able to go back into the operating room and master another complex surgery. Loving a surgeon was too hard, and she knew that if she saw any more of him, she would fall in love with him. Or rather, even more in love.

It would be impossible not to fall for a man who satisfied every need she had in every way.

Neither one of them had said anything about continuing what they had. It was like they both knew that something so perfect couldn't last forever.

Cricket lay in bed for two days after she returned from her trip. She was feeling run-down. Her stomach was incredibly queasy. She thought it was just jet lag. But she was a frequent flyer and had experienced jet lag before. This was more than that. On her third day home, she dragged herself to the doctor. And now she was sitting in the examination room waiting for her doctor to return with the results.

"Well, Cricket—" Dr. Grey returned to the room with a smile "—you're extremely healthy. You show no signs of infections."

"A virus, then? It doesn't present like a cold or the flu. I wonder if it's a new strain."

"What you have isn't new. It has been happening to women since the dawn of time."

Cricket frowned. "I'm not following you."

"You're going to have a baby."

"Excuse me?"

"Is your period late?"

"Yes, but ever since I got back from Africa it has been irregular. Are you trying to tell me that I'm pregnant?"

"You *are* pregnant. Your ob-gyn will confirm how pregnant you are, but I'm guessing you're about six weeks."

"But I'm on birth control! I have been since I was sixteen."

"Yes, but you were traveling in a lot of developing nations where infectious diseases are very prevalent. You were given a medication as a precaution to help prevent meningitis, tuberculosis and a myriad of other diseases that could potentially be fatal. That has significantly lowered the effectiveness of your birth control."

Cricket stared at the doctor, dumbfounded, for a moment. "I—I—I can't believe it."

She had been foolish. She knew the risks of having unprotected sex, but she'd done it anyway and now she was pregnant.

She was going to be a mother.

"How do you feel about having a baby?"

She shut her eyes. "I'm shocked. Completely and utterly shocked."

"Do you want this baby?"

Her eyes flew open, and she looked at the doctor. She'd never thought she wanted children. She had come in contact with them a lot through her work. She was content to help treat them, but she'd never thought she would have a baby of her own. Something that had come from her that she would be solely responsible for. It would change her life. Change her worldview and her career. Her life would never be the same.

And she found that exciting.

"Yes, I want this baby," she said honestly. "I just didn't know it until now."

There was a knock on Elias's door that evening. His Chinese food had arrived fifteen minutes ago, so he wasn't expecting anyone. Normally he didn't like unexpected visitors, but he was hoping it was one of his friends stopping by, or even one of his siblings. He had been in a funky mood all week after another visit from his doctor. He hadn't been cleared to go back to operating. There wasn't enough strength in his hand yet, and sometimes if he overworked it, there wasn't enough feeling in it.

His doctor had scolded him once again for attempting to go back so soon after complicated hand surgery. The punch he had delivered to that guy had further damaged his hand. He didn't need to be scolded by the woman. He had berated himself enough for everyone. He couldn't work. The only thing he had worth anything in his life was out of reach.

Technically he could start treating patients again. He could diagnose colds, treat broken limbs and rashes. He could work in the ER, if he was dying to get back to work. But that put him at risk of re-injuring his hand, and then there was a chance that he might never get his strength back. His other option was to wait another six to eight weeks and try to strengthen it in therapy. It wasn't much of a choice. He hadn't spent all that time learning his specialty to give it up so soon after he had started. He'd just have to wait. He was a surgeon. That was his life.

But then he opened the door to see Cricket standing there, and he forgot all about his job. She wore a coral-colored sundress with a sprinkling of tiny white flowers on the bust and gold sandals. Her hair was loose in those big fluffy curls that he was so fond of.

She was a sight for sore eyes, and he had missed her. He didn't want to admit it, but he had missed her a lot these past five weeks. There hadn't been one day when he hadn't thought about her.

He felt himself smiling—the first time he had done so all week. He grabbed her arm and without saying a word to her pulled her inside his town house. He shut the door behind her, pushed her against it and kissed her. It wasn't a soft, controlled kiss. He swept his tongue deep inside her mouth, trying to taste all the sweetness that he had gone without for the past month.

"You're happy to see me?" she asked with closed eyes when he lifted his mouth away from her. Her body had gone completely slack against him. She was warm and soft and smelled heavenly.

He had never been so hard in his life.

"Of course I'm happy to see you. Kiss me."

She obeyed his order, and he slipped his hands up her dress, finding her underwear and pulling them down.

"Wait!" She broke the kiss. "Aren't you going to ask me why I'm here?"

"I don't care why you're here."

He sucked her lower lip into his mouth and sank his fingers into the flesh of her behind.

"I have something to tell you," she protested and moaned at the same time.

"It can wait." He freed himself from his pants.

"It can't!"

He crushed his mouth to hers and pushed his hand between her legs, feeling how slick with desire she was.

"You want this as much as I do."

"Yes," she cried.

He wrapped her legs around his waist and entered her in one hard thrust. She cursed and cried out his name.

She was so tight and wet and hot. She felt so good squeezed around him that he couldn't force himself to slow down. There was no finesse to his lovemaking. Just frenzied pumping inside her.

She bit into his shoulder. She dug her fingers into his back. She cried out his name over and over again. She was never shy when they were together, never reserved. That's why he loved being with her so much.

Her body fit just right with his.

Their thoughts meshed.

Neither one of them had experienced this type of high with another partner, and he wasn't sure he would be able to experience it again.

She orgasmed hard, squeezing so tightly around him that it spurred him to come earlier than he wanted. It took his breath away. It made him see stars and forget where he was for a moment. It was powerful sex.

She was here. In his house. In Miami. She had tracked him down. This crazy attraction wasn't one-sided, and he wasn't sure he could just let her walk away for a third time. They were going to have to keep going until the intense spark they felt burned out.

After a few minutes of recovery, he lifted her into his arms and carried her to his couch. He laid her down gently, covered her body with his and kissed her softly this time. A deep, soft, long kiss. The kiss he should have given her when she walked in, before his control had snapped into a thousand little pieces.

"What did you want to tell me?" he asked her when he finally released her lips.

"We're going to have a baby, Elias."

He had heard her. He had looked into her eyes and watched the words fall from her lips, but he wasn't sure he understood.

"What?" He scrambled off her body and sat up. "What?"

The worry returned to her eyes. He had seen it when she walked in the door, but he'd ignored it, because he had been so surprised to see her. He had been happy to see her.

She sat up and pulled her dress down to cover herself. "I'm going to have a baby."

"Are you sure it's *my* baby?"

She flinched as if he had struck her in the face. "I find that question very insulting."

He knew the words were wrong as soon as he'd said them. Of course the baby was his. He had been her only lover. "I know. I'm sorry. I—I just can't get my head around this. I thought you were on birth control."

"I was up until today. I spent a lot of time with infected individuals in developing nations. I was exposed to a myriad of diseases and given medication to prevent contracting anything. They reduced the effectiveness of my birth control."

"So you just found out today?"

"Yes. My GP informed me, and then I went right to my ob-gyn. I'm about six weeks."

Six weeks.

They had met almost six weeks ago to the day. It must have happened that first night.

Elias buried his face in his hands. He was finding it hard to catch his breath.

He was going to be a father.

His life was about to change forever. Irrevocably. He could no longer do things just because he felt like it. He could no longer come and go as he pleased. He could no longer be so damn impulsive, because his decisions wouldn't just affect him. Whatever he did from now on would have an impact on this new little life he had helped to create.

And yet, as scared as he was, the thought of having a child wasn't an unpleasant one.

He had always wanted to be a father. He wanted to be like his father.

Hardworking, loving, always there for his children. And then there was Cricket, who was beautiful and brilliant and sweet. She would be a good mother.

His gut reaction was to blame her. For trapping him. For changing his life. But how the hell could he? They had had unprotected sex. He was a doctor. He knew better! He had always been so careful. Even when he was in his last committed relationship, he had been careful. But not with Cricket. Rational thoughts ceased to exist when he was with her. All thoughts ceased to exist whenever he was near her.

"Are you healthy otherwise?"

"Yes. I had my doctor test for everything. We're both healthy."

"You're keeping the baby. There's no question about that," he said firmly.

"I very much want this baby," she said softly.

He nodded and looked down at her hands, which she held tightly clasped on her lap.

"There's more I think you should know," she said gravely.

His head snapped up. He couldn't think of anything else important that he needed to know right now. He could barely wrap his head around his impending fatherhood. "What else could there be?"

"Have you ever heard of Jerome Warren?"

"The inventor and tech genius."

"He's my father."

It took a full moment for that to sink in. She wasn't just the mother of his unborn child—she was an heiress to a billion-dollar fortune. That wasn't even including the assets of her father's company, which was so successful it was dizzying.

Normally if he had learned that a woman he was dating was an heiress, it would make him pause, but it wasn't Cricket's father that he was concerned about.

"Your father is married to Dr. Frances Lundy. She's my boss. She's chief of surgery at my hospital."

"I know. She happens to be my mother," she said so quietly that he had to strain to hear her. "I should have told you sooner."

"What!" he exploded and propelled himself off the couch. "You knew I worked for your mother and you didn't say a damn thing to me?"

"I didn't know at first."

"But you sure as hell found out when I told you. Your mother already thinks I'm reckless, and now she's going to fire me when she finds out that I got you pregnant. Do you realize how important my career is to me? It's the only thing I have, and you put it in even more jeopardy by not telling me who you really are. She's never going to let me head up the trauma unit now."

"I don't know what to say."

"There's nothing to say now. Six weeks ago is when you should have opened your mouth."

"Would you have stayed away if I had?"

He paused. Would he have stayed away? Could he have stayed away? He wasn't sure. "I don't know. But I would have had the option to." He paced away from her. "I cannot believe this."

"You sound more upset about this than the baby."

"I'm not upset about the baby! You should know me better than that by now, but apparently I don't know anything about you."

"Yes, you do. You spent an entire week with me. I told you everything about myself."

"Except who your parents are."

"You liked me for me! Do you realize how rare that is for me? My father is a billionaire. The entire world knows that it's all coming to me one day, and people treat me differently because of it. The only people I can trust are in my field, because they don't care about the money. But everyone on the outside who knows looks at me as if I have dollar signs on my forehead. But you didn't do that."

"I don't care about your money. I have plenty of my own. And I don't give a damn about who your father is. He could be a postal worker or a garbage collector, for all I care. It's your mother that I'm more concerned with. What is she going to think?"

"I've been trying not to think about it." Cricket pulled her lower lip between her teeth. "I find her terrifying when she's angry. I'm more scared about telling her than I was to tell you."

Elias sat down heavily next to her, his arm pressed against hers. This whole situation was bad. He was beyond angry. His career was in serious jeopardy, but he found her damn irresistible in that moment. He couldn't stop himself from touching her. "She is terrifying," he agreed. "How are we going to break the news?"

"I'm supposed to be meeting them here for dinner in two days."

He looked up at her, and without thinking he said, "Then I guess that means we'll have to get married tomorrow afternoon."

## Chapter 5

Cricket caught a glimpse of her reflection in Elias's large bay window as she walked by. They had just gotten back from the courthouse. She was a married woman. A wife. A soon-to-be mother. She had someone else's happiness to consider now.

Elias had insisted that she get a new dress for the day. She was planning to wear one of the simple dresses she'd packed for this trip, but Elias was adamant that she have something new. Something she felt special in.

*It would be nice to start our new lives in something new.*

She had settled on a blush-colored tea-length gown with a fluffy tulle skirt. It was whimsical and pretty and fit her perfectly. If it were any other day, she might have been overjoyed with it, but it wasn't the type of dress she'd thought she would wear on her wedding day.

But then again, she'd also never thought she would be pregnant and marrying a man she barely knew.

The joy was missing from the day. The hope. The overwhelming rush of love between them.

She couldn't gauge how Elias was feeling, but she was feeling quite low. He had told her that she was beautiful that day. He had given her the most perfect ring. A round diamond set in a rose-gold band that was decorated with delicate flowers, each with a tiny diamond set in the middle. And after they were pronounced married, he kissed her sweetly on the lips, but he hadn't said a word to her since then. Not a single word on the car ride home. Nothing since they arrived back at his house.

It made that little seed of doubt in her mind bloom into a full-blown plant.

She had balked at the idea of marriage when he first brought it up last night. These were modern times. She made more than enough money on her own to support herself and her child. And with her trust fund, she could hire an army of nannies if she wanted to. But Elias had wanted this. And some foolish thing inside her made her want to give him what he wanted.

*This is important to me. Family is important to me. Marriage is important to me, and I want to show my child that. I want us to present a united front when our baby comes into the world. I know it sounds old-fashioned, but I need the mother of my child to be my wife.*

She relented. If it didn't work, they could both move on, but Cricket knew she would be hurt when it ended. There would be no way to avoid it. She had wanted to marry for love, and she was positive her husband did not love her.

She watched him as he put the paperwork they had received at the courthouse in a wall safe hidden behind a painting. He looked incredibly handsome today. Dashing, really, in a three-piece gray pinstripe suit that formed to his muscular body perfectly.

She didn't know what to do with herself now. She hadn't planned for this. When she came here yesterday, she had planned to just tell him and then retreat to the tiny apartment she kept in the city as he processed the news. But she showed up and before she could speak he was making fast, furious love to her against the door.

Sex was always incredible with him, but last night had felt different. He'd looked so happy to see her. He'd kissed her like he had missed her, and that had given her a tiny spark of hope. But today she couldn't read him. She would give anything just to know what was going on inside his head.

"Thank you for asking the man to take a picture of us. I would have never thought of that."

"I thought we needed to have at least one photo of us today."

"I love my ring." She fiddled with the band. "Have I told you that? I've never seen anything like it."

He just nodded.

"I wasn't expecting it."

"What kind of man would I be if I didn't give my wife a wedding ring?"

"You know, diamond rings weren't given before the 1930s, when a diamond company put out a large ad campaign. Diamonds aren't at all rare and are intrinsically worthless. You would be no less manly if you took your money and put a down payment on a house or invested it."

"Nerd," he said softly. "You took the romance right away with all your facts."

She smiled at him, glad that a bit of the tension was lessened. She was nervous, and when she got that way she spit out a bunch of useless facts. "I'm glad you gave me this ring. It makes the little romantic girl in me swoon."

He nodded again, and she felt so frustrated that she wanted to scream.

"I'm going to take off this suit."

"Oh. Maybe I should take off this dress, too. But I can wait until you're done."

"You don't have to wait. Come on." He led the way to his bedroom, where she had slept with him last night. Maybe *slept* was the wrong word, because she was sure that neither of them had gotten any sleep at all. She liked his place. It was what she would expect from a bachelor doctor.

It was masculine, neat and tastefully decorated with two bedrooms and an office. They could easily live there with the baby. They were probably going to have to live there once he went back to work. She would never see him otherwise. It was something they needed to talk about. It was one of the dozen things they needed to discuss.

He sat on his bed to remove his shoes and socks. She watched him for a moment, still unable to wrap her head around the fact that he was her husband.

"Do you want to go out for dinner tonight? I can cook if you don't. Or we can just order in."

"It doesn't matter to me. Whatever you want." He continued to remove his clothes. His suit coat and shirt, revealing that smooth bare chest that made her lose her train of thought.

"This is not about whatever I want. This is about you and me now and the decisions we make together."

"Really? The past twenty-four hours have felt like it has been all about you and your choices."

"Don't." She came to stand before him at the bed. "Don't you dare put this off on me. I didn't do this to you. I didn't plan this. I wasn't trying to trap you. We're going to have a baby, and you wanted to marry me. If you don't want this, tell me right now. We can get an annulment and I can take my baby to the other side of the country and you'll never have to see us again."

"Are you threatening to keep my child away from me?"

"No! I married you, Elias. If that doesn't tell you

that I want you to be in our baby's life, then I don't know what will. But I won't be the one you take this out on. I won't allow you to ice me out. I deserve better than that. So if you need space from me, let me know. Because I can be happy with or without you. The ball is in your court."

He looked up at her, and there was hurt in his eyes and maybe some fear. She only recognized those emotions because she was feeling the same way, too.

He placed his hands on her waist, pulling her closer so that he could rest his face on her belly, on their unborn child. "I don't want space from you," he said.

"What do you want?"

"Right now?" He spun her around and unzipped her dress. "I want to take my wife to bed."

She wanted to say no, to refuse him and stomp off, but she couldn't. She liked being with him. She liked his scent and the feel of his arms around her. He made her feel good in a way that no one else could, and she knew she could make him feel good in return.

He removed her strapless bra, and she was standing before him in just a pair of nude-colored underwear. "Sometimes I think the only thing you like about me is what's between my legs."

"That's not true at all." He kissed her still-flat tummy, which she found incredibly sweet. "I like other parts of your body, too." He covered her nipple with his mouth, sucking lightly on it. She suppressed a moan. Things always heated up so quickly between them, and she couldn't blame him for losing control because she was right there with him. "You have the most perfect breasts that I've ever seen," he told her right before he switched to the other nipple.

"They're big."

He looked up at her, a little mischief in his eyes. "Do you think that's a problem for me?"

"They were the cause of my teenage insecurities and frustration. I used to wear three bras just to keep them under control."

"Don't do that." He slid his hand up to one of them and squeezed lightly. "You are so damn beautiful. Do you think I would marry an ugly woman?"

"If she was having your baby, yes."

"Do you think I would get an ugly woman pregnant?"

"Yes. If you liked her very much. I don't want to think the father of my child is a shallow man. And you're not shallow. There are so many wonderful things about you. And the ability to make me feel good after I wanted to repeatedly poke you with a fork is one of them."

He smiled at her, a real smile, and the fist around her heart loosened. He stood up and kissed her forehead. "I like what's in here, too." He pulled down her underwear and ordered her into bed.

She obeyed and lay in the center of his big bed under the covers, watching him strip off the remainder of his clothing. She was nervous. Her heart was racing, and she felt like it was her first time with him all over again. Only this time was more momentous, because she wasn't having sex with a man she had just met. She was making love to her husband and the father of her child.

He settled on top of her, the lower half of his body in between her legs. He didn't enter her even though she'd been ready the moment he unzipped her dress. He kissed her. Long, deep, unrushed kisses that made her melt into the bed and took her breath away.

She didn't know what was going to happen between them or if this fragile marriage was going to last, but this moment was nice, this moment she would hold on to and recall when things got tough between them.

The restaurant where they were meeting Cricket's parents was one of the best in Miami. This was no casual dining establishment, and they had to dress the part. Elias wore a navy blue suit and his best pair of shoes, but Cricket was the stunner. She wore a cream-colored lace dress that fit her curvy body like a glove. It was distractingly sexy but still appropriate enough for dinner with her parents.

She was nervous. There was no denying it. He didn't blame her, because he had been dreading this meeting all day. It could make or break his future, but he was more concerned about her at the moment. He took her hand, and she looked over to him almost gratefully. He had no words for her, but he could offer his touch. They had that. If nothing else, they could take comfort in each other's bodies even if it wasn't in bed.

"This is my mother's favorite restaurant," she told him as they entered.

"Mine is the burger joint on Calloway Boulevard."

"Really?" Her eyes widened a bit. "Can we go there after we leave here? I don't think I'll be able to eat."

"Of course. You haven't eaten all day. You need to feed my child."

"I'm too nervous."

He squeezed her hand, and when that didn't seem like enough, he wrapped his arm around her and kissed her cheek.

The hostess showed them to their table. Mr. Jerome Warren and Dr. Lundy were already there. The eccentric billionaire was wearing a houndstooth-patterned sport coat and a teal bow tie. He smiled broadly when he spotted them. Dr. Lundy looked gorgeous but understated in a black cocktail dress. She didn't smile. She frowned in confusion.

"Dr. Bradley," she started. "I had you banned from my hospital, and you track my daughter down to meet with me. I don't know if it's clever or stalkerish, but you could have simply called. Though it wouldn't have made a difference. I got the report from your orthopedist. You haven't been cleared to return to surgery yet."

"We're not here on account of my career tonight."

He pulled out Cricket's chair before taking his seat beside her.

"Franny," Jerome said, "you sound like you already know Cricket's friend."

"He's not Cricket's friend. He's my top trauma surgeon, who broke his hand doing some ridiculous mud race."

"Those look like so much fun!" Mr. Warren said. "If I were younger, I would do one myself."

"You don't have to be young to do them, sir. My sister-in-law's father just did one with my brother. He had a wonderful time. I'm Elias, by the way."

"It's nice to meet you, Elias. It's an unexpected pleasure."

"What are you doing here, Doctor?" Dr. Lundy stared at him in a way that could make flowers wither.

"Mother, you were right about Elias not being my friend. He's my husband."

Elias hadn't expected Cricket to blurt it out like that, but he was glad she did. It was out in the open now.

"Your what!"

"Congratulations, honey!"

Cricket's hand crept into his, and he locked his fingers with hers.

"We're married, Dr. Lundy," Elias said. "I didn't know she was your daughter when we met."

"You're pregnant, aren't you?"

"Yes," she said softly. "I'm very happy about it. I didn't marry Elias because I'm having his baby. I married him because it felt right."

That comment made him pause. He kept asking himself why he'd asked her to marry him. The words had just popped out of his mouth.

It wasn't love. It couldn't be, and if he were in this situation with anyone else, he wouldn't have asked. But he wanted all of Cricket. Marrying her felt like the right thing to do. He was the first man to make love to her. He had given her a baby. He felt like he needed to be her husband.

"I knew you wanted to be head of trauma, but I didn't think you would stoop this low. You seduce my daughter, get her pregnant and marry her! You thought this was going to force my hand?"

"I don't care if you have a low opinion of me, but your daughter is no naive dupe. Even if I was so evil, Cricket is smart enough not to get pulled in. I want the job, but I knew it was a never a guarantee. I'm a damn good surgeon, and if I could get hired at your hospital, I can get hired at another top institution. Our relationship didn't start with you in mind. In fact, I didn't even know you were her mother until two days ago."

"It's true, Mother. I knew that Elias worked for you, but he didn't know that I knew."

"He was in your home, and he had no clue who your parents were." Dr. Lundy shook her head in disgust. "I thought you had gotten smarter since your college days."

"Don't, Mother. I was seventeen!"

"It was the same story. You told us he didn't care

about who your father was. That he loved you for you, and next thing we know you were trying to cash out your savings account to buy him a car."

"I learned my lesson. I was a kid. Why can't you let that go?"

"Because now you have gotten yourself pregnant. I wish I could trust you, but I can't."

"Enough, Frances," Jerome said in a stern voice that Elias was sure no one else dared to use with Dr. Lundy. "Cricket is our only child, and she is bringing a life into this world. She is a grown woman with two doctorates who has dedicated her life to making the world a healthier place. We are inordinately proud of her, and we're *thrilled* to be grandparents. And if the man she chose to marry is a doctor that you yourself hired, he mustn't be all that bad. Instead of biting everyone's head off, take a moment to see the joy in this situation." He reached across the table and set his hand over Cricket's free one. "I can't wait to be a grandfather, honey. I prayed for you to find happiness. I'm happy for you. Congratulations."

"Thank you, Daddy." She left her chair to hug her father, and as soon as she let him go, she turned to Elias. "Can you take me home? I don't feel well." She swayed a little.

He was out of his seat in an instant, grabbing her and pulling her close to him. "What's the matter, baby?" he asked as she clung to him.

He was worried about her. She hadn't eaten all day because she was nervous about how this evening was going to go. It had gone as badly as one could expect, and he wanted to take her away from here. He wanted to protect her from her mother's vitriol that was partially his fault. If he were any other man, he knew it wouldn't have gone so poorly. But he wasn't any other man. He was her husband now, and Dr. Lundy was just going to have to get over it. Being head of trauma was his dream, but he had a family now. His father had always put them first. Elias was going to do the same for his family. His father would have been disappointed in him if he led his life any other way.

"Can you make it to the car or should I carry you out?"

"You already broke your hand. Do you think I want to be the cause of your broken back? You'll never operate again. No, thank you. I can't live with that kind of guilt."

He grinned. He couldn't help it. He kissed her cheek. He couldn't help that, either. "Let's get out of here."

"Hamburgers," she whispered into his ear.

"Anything you want."

## Chapter 6

When they got back to Elias's town house, he ordered her to bed. She wasn't used to anyone ordering her about, and the independent woman in her wanted to bristle. But she was too tired and numb, and frankly it was a little nice to have someone else to think for her when she couldn't manage to herself. He was protective. He might not have married her for love, but he was going to take his duty as a husband seriously.

He had promised her a hamburger, and she thought he was going to run out to get dinner. But a few minutes later, the doorbell rang and he walked into the bedroom with a greasy bag that looked large enough to hold food for a small army of people.

"Smells like heaven." She sighed as she kicked off her shoes. Her lower back was aching in a way that it never had before, and suddenly she felt too tired to eat. "When did you order it?"

"I have an app on my phone. It took less than two minutes."

She struggled to unzip her dress, but then she felt large warm hands on her back and soon his knuckles were pressed against her bare skin as he unzipped.

"Do you want me to get you something to sleep in?" he asked, knowing that most of her clothes were in Hideaway Island, because she hadn't planned to still be here. She especially hadn't planned to marry him today.

"No, thank you. I think I should eat first."

"You should. I was worried about you," he told her as she sat down heavily on his bed.

"Don't be. Fainting and dizziness are a sign of early pregnancy. So is lower-back pain." She propped up the pillows behind her, making a mental note to make sure she got some more for the bed.

"Rationally and medically I know that, but still, when it's your wife and your child, you can't help but worry."

She found his words sweet, but there was still some of that awkward tension between them that had been there most of the day. The only time it had disappeared was when they walked into the restaurant as a united front. But now that they were alone again, it returned.

Part of her wondered if part of him thought she had done this to him on purpose. Women trapped successful men all the time. And ever since he found out that she was hiding the truth about who her mother was, he didn't trust her.

But after tonight, who could blame him?

"I'm going to feed you well tonight." He sat next to her on his bed. Technically their bed, but she wasn't sure if it was ever going to feel like she belonged there. "I'm going to advise against eating like this throughout your pregnancy. But tonight I say we make an exception. We deserve it." He began unloading the bag. "I wasn't sure what kind of loaded fries you'd prefer, so I got buffalo chicken and bacon and just plain old cheese and bacon–loaded fries. There's cheeseburgers in there. I normally get mine with everything on it, but I had them put everything on the side for you because I don't know how you like your burgers yet. There's onion rings. A slice of chocolate cake, a piece of apple pie and I left the milkshakes in the living room."

"I could cry," Cricket said to him. "This is a heart attack in a paper bag, but it's so beautiful I could cry."

"You are crying," he said quietly as he wiped a tear from her cheek with his thumb.

"Am I? I'm sorry. It must be the pregnancy hormones."

"Don't apologize. You're tired and hungry, and we just had a very tense meeting with your parents. It's okay to be upset."

"I feel like we should talk about it."

"I feel like you need to feed my baby first."

He handed her the container with her cheeseburger, and she absently loaded it with every fixing that was in there. "You keep saying *your* baby. You're quite possessive over something that is going to come out of my body in a very painful manner."

"I know." He flashed her that devastatingly gorgeous grin of his. "That's the best part of being a father. All of the glory. None of the excruciating pain."

She laughed, still feeling the tears run down her face. She didn't feel particularly sad, but she couldn't stop them.

"Eat." He leaned over and kissed the side of her face and let his lips linger there. "You'll feel better after you do."

She shut her eyes, willing him to keep his lips on her skin. It reminded her that she was no longer alone in this world. There was a time in her life when she'd never thought she would have a family of her own, and now she was going to have one. It might not be the way she'd dreamed of but it was a family all the same. She had been alone for years. It was nice not to feel that way anymore.

"So you like your burgers with everything on them, too?"

"Not usually. But tonight if you hand me a can of cold gravy, I would pile that on top, too."

They ate mostly in silence with his large-screen television on in the background, but Elias sat close to her, their sides pressed together. She found his presence comforting, even with the heavy silence surrounding them.

When they were done, he removed all of the food from the room, leaving her with just a milkshake.

She knew she should get up and take off her fancy dress, but she was too tired to stand. So she sat on the bed, her hands folded over her belly, and thought about the life growing inside her. The life her mother was very upset about.

It was too soon to know the sex of the baby she was carrying, but she kept thinking it might be a boy. She hoped he looked just like Elias with his beautiful black curls and his strong build.

"Cricket…" Elias gathered her into his arms and held her tightly against him. "I don't like to see you upset."

She was crying again. She hadn't realized she'd started, but the hot tears splashing down her cheeks told her she was.

"She'll come around. It will be okay."

"I'm so happy about this baby. She acts like I'm ruining my life."

"She's mad about me. She thinks I'll ruin your life."

"Any other mother would be thrilled that I came home married to a gorgeous surgeon."

"You think I'm gorgeous?"

She gave him a wobbly smile. "I only have sex with gorgeous men. Makes for better-looking kids."

The corner of his mouth curled. "She thinks I'm using you to get ahead in my career."

"You aren't devious. I know that."

"I'm glad you do. But the truth is, you don't know me that well. I could be a ton of things."

"You don't know me well, either. But you married me."

"I needed to."

Because of the baby. Not because he was fond of her or thought he could love her. He'd married her because he felt he had no other choice. It didn't make her feel very good about their chances in that moment.

"Help me get out of this dress?" She stood up, feeling a little wobbly, and went to his side of the bed. "It's too tight. Can you pull the top down?"

"Yes." He did as she asked, and she couldn't help but notice that he touched her more than necessary while he did. He didn't just pull her arms out of the sleeves. His fingers slid across her shoulders and skidded down her back. The dress was tight on her hips and he had to yank it down, but he took her underwear with it.

His lips grazed her lower back, and every nerve ending in her body screamed for more. "Do you want to have sex now?"

"No. We're both exhausted and full. I just want to touch you."

"But I'm willing." She turned around and looked down into his eyes. There was arousal there. She loved when he looked at her like she was the sexiest thing ever created.

"You don't have to have sex with me because it's your wifely duty."

"I know." She lifted his hand and placed it between her legs, inside her lips so that he could feel her moisture.

"Spread your legs a little more."

She did.

"Kiss me."

She did that, too, and took so much pleasure in it. He just touched, slowly working his fingers in her folds. His pace should have slowed down the climax; instead his gentle touch brought it on quick and hard. She was crying out and breathless, and as soon as she had shuddered for the last time, he stood up, scooped her into his arms and placed her on the bed on her belly. He unhooked her bra, and she was expecting him to turn her over and cover her body with his and push inside her, but he didn't. She smelled lightly scented lotion and then felt his big hot hands on her back.

It was sweet. It was perfect. She felt like weeping again. But she held back. "Talk to me, Elias."

"About what?"

"About us. About anything. I think we have so much to say to each other."

"But where to start?"

"What do you want out of life?"

"I wanted that job. I wanted to be head of trauma. I wanted to eventually head up my own hospital."

"But now?"

"I just want to do the right thing."

"Oh."

"I like Miami Mercy. I liked working for your mother, but if you want me to quit that hospital, I will. I can find another job someplace else. We might have to move out of the state, but I will leave if you want me to."

She was touched by the offer, but she couldn't ask him to do that. She was already holding on to the guilt that she had made him marry a woman he didn't love. She hadn't actually made him propose, but she should have said no, should have stood firm and made him see reason.

"I don't want you to leave." She didn't want to do anything that would make him unhappy.

"This is a premature conversation. I'm still not allowed to go back to work. It will be at least another six to eight weeks."

"You had another appointment since I last saw you. You weren't cleared to go back?"

"I wasn't expecting to be. Wishful thinking on my part. I knew that it was going to be at least six months because of my specialty. I couldn't just fracture my wrist—I had to break the hell out of it. I live my life doing just a little bit too much," he said as his strong hands traveled down her back.

"Comminuted fracture?" she asked, but it came out as a moan.

"Yes." He kissed her shoulder. "Extra-articular displaced." He lifted her hair to kiss the back of her neck. "I've never dated a woman who knew her medical terms so well."

"It turns you on that I know that you broke your bone in more than two pieces?"

"Yes. Your brainy medical knowledge is the reason I married you."

"You married me because you impregnated me."

"That was a very small factor in my decision." He was quiet for a moment as he continued to massage her back. "I don't regret asking you to marry me, you know." It was as if he was reading her mind.

"We've only been married for twenty-four hours. Give it a few weeks."

"You're easy to be with, Cricket."

"I'm sorry about today."

"It was just one bad half hour. The whole day wasn't bad. I like your father," he said, changing the subject as he focused his hands on her lower back. "How often does a man get to meet a billionaire?"

"My father is pretty wonderful. He was born in the Deep South. Poorer than piss and turnips, as he is fond of saying, and then he pulled himself up."

"He is self-made. Just like your mother."

"That's what they have in common. They both made everything out of nothing. She thinks I have it easier than they did, and I do in hundreds of ways, but my life hasn't been easy. I worked hard, too. My mother thinks I have wasted my potential."

"You have two doctorates. You're well respected in your field."

"My mother says while my nose is in a book, real doctors are out actually solving problems."

"And now I get your issues with surgeons. I thought you were just stereotyping us. You were speaking about your mother."

"Yes. I'll stop complaining about my mother now. It must be really sexy to have a complaining, weepy pregnant woman in your bed."

"If you could see what I scc, you wouldn't doubt why I have you in my bed."

"Lie down with me," she said to him as she slipped off her loosened bra.

"Okay." She watched him as he stripped down to just his underwear. She knew she would never tire of looking at his body. He was so beautifully built. Her own body was about to go through a massive change, and she wondered if he still would want to touch her after it did. Their bodies were what kept them connected. What kind of marriage would they have when he was no longer attracted to her?

"Take everything off, please."

He slid his underwear down, revealing his manhood, which was nearly fully erect and gently bobbing as he looked at her.

"Let me love you," she said, reaching out to him.

He took her hand and slid into bed beside her. "I don't think I could stop you."

## Chapter 7

A week after the revelation to Cricket's parents, they returned to Hideaway Island. Elias had been planning to go back briefly for a family function, but Cricket asked him to stay on the island until he was cleared to go back to work. She had been afraid to ask him, he could tell. He still remembered the look on her face when she approached him. All flustered and adorable.

*I—I don't want to interrupt your life any more, but would you mind if—if we lived on Hideaway until you go back to work? Or at least go back on the weekends. If you don't want to go, I could go by myself. But I would like you to come. That is, if you want to.*

He'd wanted to kiss her right then, take her to bed

and peel her clothes off and spend a few hours just buried inside her body. But he didn't. He just agreed to go back with her. Elias was never the type of man who had vices. He drank responsibly. He never gambled. He didn't chase after women. But Cricket had turned on something inside him that made him want to touch her. All the time. Be with her every second of the day, and there were a lot of times when he had to hold himself back. Prevent himself from touching her. He didn't want her to think that all he thought about was sex. He wouldn't blame her if she did, because their relationship had started because they couldn't keep their hands off each other.

He still couldn't keep his hands off her, but he liked her, too. He liked her smile and her voice and the nerdy things she said. He liked that she was his and no one else could claim her.

He saved his passion for her until night fell, and then he loved her for hours. There were times when he tried to give her a break and let her rest for a night or two, but she wasn't content to sleep. She would reach for him, or touch him or simply look his way, and he needed to have her.

*Needed* to.

It was more than a want.

Much more.

"Are you sure I look okay today?" she asked him, worry in her eyes. She'd often seemed unsure of herself during their short marriage. Like she was afraid to upset him. She wanted to make sure he was happy.

He wanted to reassure her, but he didn't know how. He didn't know how to be married, and in the end, he knew it was his job to make sure she was happy, too.

"You're beautiful." He grabbed her hips and kissed along her jaw. He felt her relax a little. "It's just a barbecue with my family. Stop being so skittish."

She wore a short white dress with multicolored sailboats on it and cobalt blue sandals. She had left her hair down at his request. It probably made more sense for her to wear it up in the humid Florida heat, but it was one of those little things she did to please him. She had no idea that she pleased him without even trying.

"They don't know about us," she said, wrapping her arms around him.

"They'll find out today."

"What if they hate me?"

"Why would they hate you?"

"Because I got pregnant and stole you away from all the other eligible bachelorettes on the planet."

"You didn't get pregnant on purpose."

She looked up at him, the worry not leaving her eyes. "I know, but what if they think that?"

"Then I'll tell them you're an heiress and that I married you for your money."

"Good plan." She smiled briefly and then looked up at him for a long moment, her lips opened as if she were about to speak, but she remained silent.

"Tell me."

"It was nothing."

"Tell me," he insisted.

"Kiss me."

He set his hands on her cheeks and kissed her softly. It was a controlled kiss, because he knew if he let himself really kiss her, he would go wild. She was pregnant. She was his wife. He couldn't go around making love to her on the sides of bathtubs and against walls, no matter how satisfying it might be.

"I want to have scx in the middle of the day," she said, shocking the hell out of him.

"Excuse me?"

"I would like to do that sometimes," she blurted out. "A lot, actually. I need you to do it with me."

"And if I'm unavailable, will you get someone else?"

She blinked at him. "Well, I called that gigolo, but he's booked up for the next six weeks. I guess when you're good at your job, everyone wants you."

She made him laugh. Whenever any inkling of doubt crept into his mind, she would say something unexpected that would make him laugh and want her even more. "Lucky for you I'm available."

"Lucky for me."

"I'll make love to you at twelve fifteen."

"Don't tell me when. Surprise me. Surprise me often, if you can."

She had no idea what she was doing to him, giving him this kind of permission to access her body.

He could get drunk off her and happily stay that way for the rest of his life. "Okay." He nodded, not at all sure if other newly married couples spoke to each other this way. "We need to go now."

She nodded and gave him one more kiss before she let him go.

His brother, Carlos, lived on the far side of the island, in a section that was so secluded it felt like part of another country. The landscape was wilder—tall grasses and big colorful flowers lined the ocean-side road that led there. Elias loved the house, especially after his sister-in-law, Virginia, finished decorating it. But it was a little too far away from town for his tastes. He thought he would never be able to survive living outside a major city, but he had agreed to stay on Hideaway with Cricket until he went back to work. He was looking forward to his time on the island with her. He had been feeling stuck the past month before she reentered his life. Now he had been drop-kicked out of his restlessness and into a more terrifying life.

"Elias, is there something you need to tell me?" she asked as they pulled into Carlos's long driveway.

"No."

"No? I'm an heiress to one of the biggest fortunes in the country, and even I have never seen a house this big."

She was right. Her house was nice, but Carlos's house was amazing by anyone's standards.

"I told you that my brother was a baseball player."

"I thought you meant in school."

"You mean you never realized that my brother is Carlos Bradley?"

"I'm sorry," she said in nearly a whisper. "I have no idea who he is."

"Shortstop for the Miami Hammerheads. Played twenty seasons for the same team. He's a legend and one of the most recognizable athletes on the planet. Hell, the president honored him."

"I'm sorry," she said again, looking at her hands. "I don't know who he is."

Elias pulled his car to a stop, threw back his head and laughed. Of course she didn't know who his brother was. She read scientific journals for fun. She barely watched television, and when she did, it almost always was some sort of documentary. It made sense. He had married the only woman on the planet who didn't care who he was related to. It was refreshing.

"Why is that so funny?"

"Because I've had women try to get with me just because my brother is my brother."

"Why? What do you have to do with him?"

"They're social climbers and status seekers. They thought I would lead them to him."

"But you're a doctor. You work at some of the most prestigious hospitals in the country. You're beautiful. They surely wouldn't think your brother was more worthy just because he hits a ball with a wooden stick. You save lives."

"You haven't met my brother yet. Carlos is very good-looking. He's very rich and he's very famous. Most people would consider him the catch out of the two of us. But he's also very married to the love of his life, so women settle for me."

"Some women are stupid." She stepped out of the car, seeming annoyed on his behalf. He was glad for it. It meant she was no longer nervous.

He joined her, and together they made the walk from the driveway to the huge house. It was a Spanish-style mansion, painted a cream color, with a roof made of handcrafted red tiles. They stood in front of the heavy carved wood door waiting for someone to open it. It didn't matter how many times he had been here; Elias was still blown away that someone in his family lived in a place like this. They had grown up working-class, in a tiny three-bedroom house. Their parents had worked two jobs each. They probably all still would have gone to school and made something of themselves because their parents valued education that much, but Carlos had made things easier for them. It was because of his brother that Elias wasn't drowning in student-loan debt. He owed him a great deal, but whenever Elias tried to pay him back, Carlos refused. Carlos didn't get to go to college because he was drafted right out of high school, but he'd wanted to make sure his siblings got every ounce of schooling they wanted. Elias wanted to make him proud, and he really wanted Carlos to like Cricket. Elias wanted his entire family to like Cricket. But in the long run it wouldn't make a damn bit of difference if they did or not. He had married her. She was carrying his child. So their opinion of her wouldn't change a thing.

"Let's not lead with the marriage thing this time," he said to her. "We should tell them later in the day. I don't want to make today about us."

"I don't want to ruin two occasions this month."

"You didn't ruin anything," he said as the door swung open. His twin sister was the one to answer it. Her eyes went wide when she saw he wasn't alone.

"Oh! Hi!" She smiled warmly at them. Ava had been known as somewhat of an ice goddess before she met her husband. Marriage had mellowed her out. She was almost like a new person. Elias had always loved his twin more than anyone else on the planet, and now he really liked her, too. "I didn't know you were bringing anyone."

"Who's bringing someone?" Carlos appeared, holding his now-two-year-old daughter. "Elias?" Both his siblings were surprised to see Cricket standing with him. They gave him curious identical looks. He had never brought anyone home. Not since his first serious girlfriend in med school.

"I know who you are now!" Cricket exclaimed, looking at Carlos. "I used to see you every day from my office window in Boston. You're the pizza guy."

"I'd like to think of myself as a fourteen-time all-star and World Series champion, but yes, I was the spokesman for Pippa's Pizzas," he said with a grin.

"Cricket had no clue who you are," Elias explained. "I think she's more excited about the pizza connection than the baseball."

"Pizza?" Carlos's daughter said from his arms.

"Not today, baby." He looked at his daughter with pure love that only a parent could give to a child. "We've got good stuff for you to eat." His eyes went back to Cricket. "This is my daughter, Bria."

"Hello, Bria. I love your pretty dress."

"Pink flowers," she said, looking down at her outfit.

Elias saw Cricket's heart go into her eyes as she looked at his niece, and it once again hit him that they were going to have a baby. In about seven months, they were going to have something special that was going to bond them together for life.

"I'm Cricket, by the way," she said, looking up at Carlos and Ava. "It's very nice to meet you. Elias has told me wonderful things about you both."

"I'm glad my brother hasn't forgotten about us. Elias hasn't told us a thing about you. If fact, he has been extremely quiet these past two months," Ava said, looking at him with some annoyance. "But I'm very glad that we are meeting today. If he brought you to meet us, you must be special." Ava gave him a genuine smile.

"Yes. It's nice to meet you, Cricket," Carlos said. "Please come inside. We're just about ready to fire up the grill."

They walked out to the outdoor living room,

which overlooked a huge pool and the ocean. His sister-in-law was with her mother at the table setting out fruit-filled drinks. Virginia turned around and looked up at them and so did her mother. It was then Elias heard ear-shattering, happy feminine screams.

"Dr. Warren! You get over here and give me a hug, young lady," Dr. Andersen said, beaming.

"Dr. Andersen! I'm so happy to see you. You look incredible."

The two women hugged, and the rest of them looked puzzled. "Your girlfriend knows my mother-in-law?" Carlos muttered.

"Very well, it seems," Elias said, watching the two women embrace.

"And did I hear her correctly? She's a Dr. Warren?"

"Two PhDs. Biology and cultural anthropology. She mostly does medical research, but she's an author, too. She's working on her fourth book."

"Oh, yes, Carlos. You have to read Cricket's books," Dr. Andersen said, looping her arm around Cricket and walking over to them. "Cricket studies how diseases affect cultures and relationships. *Mourning in the Developing Nations* kept me up at night. It made me weep. This girl is brilliant."

"If my mother-in-law gives that kind of endorsement, it must be true. I'm taking anthropology this semester," he said to Cricket.

"Are you!" Cricket's eyes widened in excitement. "Please, tell me you like it."

"It's just the intro class, but I'm finding it fascinating."

"I'm giving a lecture in Miami in a few weeks. You must come! I'll be showing slides from my trip this summer to India. I was studying a village of sex workers who were all infected—"

"You were what?" Elias nearly shouted.

"You knew about that."

"Not the sex worker part."

"They were very nice ladies. Most of them weren't more than girls, though."

"I'm more concerned about the men who visit them."

"I was fine," she said, and he didn't believe her.

"I think we need to talk about this some more later." He didn't want her going back there. Hell, he didn't want her going any other place where people were infected with diseases for the rest of her life.

"Cricket's work is important, Elias," Dr. Andersen said lightly. "And I take it by the disapproving tone and the scowl on your face that you two are a couple."

"Yes." He reached for her hand.

"I'll definitely come to your lecture. You want to come with, Mama Andersen?" Carlos asked his mother-in-law.

"Nothing would make me happier."

A few hours later, the party was in full swing. Ava was married to the mayor of the island, and he brought his entire family over. There were a few kids running around and splashing in the pool. Food was abundant, drinks were flowing. There was a nice ocean breeze.

"This is what Dad envisioned when he saw this place," Carlos said from beside him.

"I know. I wish he could be here to see it."

"I think he is."

Cricket appeared in his line of vision wearing a white bikini. She was walking toward him, like she was out of a dream. The only way he could describe her was womanly. Smooth hips, thick thighs and large, lush breasts. He didn't even notice the other women with her until they approached.

Without a word she reached for him, wrapping her arms around him and pressing her curvy body into his. He smoothed his hand down the curve of her back, forcing himself to stop before he cupped her backside in his hands. He was aroused, and he wanted her so badly it hurt. But that's how he felt every minute of every day.

"Tell me I look awful and that you want me to put my clothes back on," she said into his ear.

"I would never say that to you. And if I do, you should leave me. You're the sexiest thing I've ever seen."

She pressed a kiss to his mouth before she spoke in his ear again. "Your brother is very handsome, but you make my heart beat faster."

"Meet me in the house in fifteen minutes," he

whispered. "Down the long hallway on the first floor. Second door on the right."

Her eyes went wide. "No."

"You said surprise you."

"No," she said again.

"Come on, Cricket," Hallie, Virginia's sister-in-law, called to her. "The beach is calling us."

She gave Elias one last shy smile before she went off.

"Can you believe it took us fifteen minutes to convince your girlfriend to leave the house wearing that bathing suit? She wanted to wear a T-shirt over it!" Ava exclaimed. "I didn't think bodies like hers existed in the real world. You should have seen my husband's eyes pop out of his head when she walked by. But how can I blame him? Even I can't stop staring at her butt."

"I'm going to have to agree with her," Virginia said. "That body is spectacular, right, babe?" she asked her husband.

"No comment," he said smartly.

"It's okay." Virginia grinned at him. "You can admit it. I want to paint her nude. It would fit in my next series featuring all-natural bodies." She looked at Elias. "Do you think it would be weird if I asked her?"

"Yes," he said. "Very weird." Virginia was a trained painter, and her pieces sold for hundreds of thousands of dollars, but Cricket was his, and as selfish as it was, he didn't want anyone else to have her.

"I didn't get it before," Carlos said. "She's adorable and smart and I like her a lot, but I didn't get why you two were together. She's not your usual type, but I get it now. Damn."

"Do you like her, Ava?" Elias asked his twin. He held his breath as he waited for her answer.

"Very much so. She's fascinating and very sweet and makes me feel a little dumb, but I could see us becoming friends."

"Virginia?" he asked.

"I'm pretty sure my mother wishes that she was her daughter instead of me, so I'm mortally jealous of her, but other than that I find her charming. She wouldn't happen to be the daughter of Jerome Warren, would she?"

"The guy who invented every gadget in our house?" Carlos asked. "The billionaire?"

Elias nodded. "He's a really nice guy."

"Wait a minute." Ava shook her head. "Didn't you tell me your boss was married to him? You're dating your boss's daughter?"

"No. I married my boss's daughter," he told them.

They all went silent, their faces revealing their shock. He hadn't planned how he was going to break the news, but all day they'd kept calling Cricket his girlfriend. She was more than that. She was the woman he had promised to spend the rest of his life with. She was going to be the mother of his child. His family needed to know.

"She's your wife?" Ava shook her head.

"We met here on the island and I couldn't leave her that first night. And then when I did leave her, I couldn't stop thinking about her, so I saw her again. I stayed for an entire week."

"That's when you told me you were taking a trip," Ava said. "I thought you were in California, but Derek said he was fairly sure he saw you in town."

"He did. I thought I dodged him."

"Why didn't you just tell me that you were seeing someone?"

"Cricket is someone I wanted to keep all to myself."

"So you married her?" Carlos said, sounding disbelieving.

"I needed to be married to her. There's no other way to describe it. I needed her to be my wife."

"I felt that way about Virginia," Carlos said, reaching for his wife.

"We're having a baby, too." He dropped the second bomb.

"You're going to be a father?" Virginia asked in awe.

He smiled. It might not have been the right time, but the thought of being a father made him happy. "Her mother wants to murder me. She thinks this is some plan I cooked up to propel my career forward. I might end up losing my job because of this, but I don't care. I can work at another hospital. I wouldn't be able to forgive myself if I let Cricket slip through my fingers."

He looked over at Ava, who had tears streaming down her cheeks, her chest softly heaving.

"Hey, Elias. I—" Cricket reappeared from somewhere. "Uh-oh. You told them."

Ava flung herself at Cricket and hugged her tightly. "I'm so happy for you. Welcome to the family."

Elias let out a slow breath of relief. His twin wouldn't lie about something like that. He looked at his brother, afraid of his reaction.

"We're happy for you." He smiled. "Mom is going to murder you. But we're very happy for you." Carlos came over and hugged him tightly.

His family was on board, which somehow put more pressure on him. He really couldn't allow this marriage to fail now.

## Chapter 8

Three weeks had gone by since Elias broke the news
to his family. Outwardly they had been much more
supportive than Cricket's mother. Ava and Virginia
had stopped by a few times to invite Cricket along
for shopping and out to lunch. They were making an
effort to include her in the family. It was unexpect-
edly kind. Their unfaltering excitement about having a new sister seemed genuine. Cricket, who was
an only child and had never had many friends, felt
warmed by it. But in the back of her mind, she wondered how they truly felt.

Didn't they think it was too soon? That she and
Elias couldn't possibly be in love after such a short

period of time? That they were bringing a baby into this world and they were still practically strangers?

Those thoughts had to be going through their minds, because they were still going through Cricket's. But neither one of them showed any signs of doubt, because she knew Elias had sold their marriage to them as uncontrollable love, that they couldn't be apart and that their baby was just a happy bonus. Ava told her that she had never heard her brother say anything so beautiful before as when he spoke about her.

But Cricket didn't feel any closer to her husband. They made love every night, more than once. She wanted to be near him. She wanted to touch him. She wanted to look at his handsome face all day, but she kept herself away. She claimed she had to work on her book, which she did, but she wasn't getting very far. She couldn't concentrate on what was going on in pockets of the world thousands of miles away when she didn't know how to handle what was going on in her own home.

She didn't want Elias to think she was clingy. That she had gotten pregnant to trap him. She didn't want anyone to think that, but she was a trained medical professional. She knew the side effects of the medications she was taking. She should have known not to have sex with him without more protection. But she'd never thought he would walk into her world. She'd never thought he would want to marry her. And if she had to do it all over again, she knew she wouldn't change a thing. She wanted this baby. Even though she knew what she was up against. Even though she was sure her relationship with her mother was never going to be the same.

"Hey." Elias came into her office and lay on the couch adjacent to her desk.

"Hey." She spun around in her chair. He rarely came to see her during the day. She knew he was bored here, but she didn't know how to remedy it. She was afraid the only thing that would satisfy him was going back to work as a surgeon.

She remembered how restless and irritable her mother had been when she was out after a knee replacement. She could only imagine how restless Elias was. He was in his prime. He loved to work. Finding ways to fill his time was hard for him.

"Can I come sit next to you?" she asked him, wishing she could be easier around him.

"You can always sit next to me." He sat up, making space for her on the couch. He took her hand when she sat. He locked his fingers with hers, and she felt like she did when she was still a girl, when that first boy made her feel special. "How's the book coming?"

"Not great. I'm a little preoccupied." She touched her belly, which was starting to round ever so slightly.

"Yeah." He covered her hand with his own. "I know what you mean. Have you spoken to your mother yet?"

"No. She texted me last week to ask me about a book, but nothing else."

"Did you really try to buy a car for some guy?"

She'd been wondering when he was going to ask her about that. She was still embarrassed by it. She was supposed to be so intelligent, but she was human and sometimes she did foolish things. "I did. After I bought him sneakers, a leather jacket and basketball tickets."

"Cricket," he groaned. "I don't want to believe that."

"Believe it." She lifted his hand to her mouth and kissed it. "You need a car? How about diamond cuff links. A gold scalpel? I'm your girl."

"Why did you do it?"

"I thought I loved him. I wanted to make him happy."

"You're enough," he said quietly.

*But am I enough for you?* she wanted to ask, but forced herself not to. "I grew up a little bit in a bubble. I didn't go to high school. My parents hired private tutors to educate me when they thought that traditional schools weren't enough. I went to college at sixteen. I was a pudgy, awkward, insecure wreck, and I was also an heiress and everyone knew it. Then Mike came along, and he was sweet to me. I was so unpopular in school, so unliked, so alone that when someone was nice to me, I jumped on it. I wanted to keep that feeling, and I gave up a little bit of myself to do so. In the back of my head I knew he was using me, but I refused to acknowledge it. It hurts to think about it, to know that I let myself be used. But it's part of my history. It has made me who I am today."

"It's also made you isolate yourself from people. People that would love you just because you are you. My sisters really love you."

She was surprised by his last statement. "What?"

"They want to be your friend. They want to be a big part of our lives. They want you to call them."

"Did I do something to offend them? I didn't mean to. I'll call them to apologize."

"You didn't do anything wrong, but they are your family now. You can trust them. They wouldn't make an effort unless they wanted to know you."

"They love you. They'll accept me because they love you. Because they are nice people."

"Don't keep yourself away because you're afraid of what others might think. Don't be afraid that they don't like you."

"It's not just anyone. I don't care about what strangers think. I care what *you* think. I care about what your family thinks. We both know that if I hadn't gotten pregnant, we never would have seen each other again. What does that say about us?"

"Who cares what it says about us? You *are* pregnant, and *I* choose to spend the rest of my life with you. And I want you to stop being so damn shy around me. I'm not just some guy who got you pregnant. I'm your husband now. And I don't want us to walk around here like we're some damn polite strangers."

"You're unhappy. I knew you were."

"You're unhappy," he countered.

"I'm not! I get nervous around you. I don't know how to behave."

"Be yourself! We spent an entire week together just three days after meeting. I couldn't leave you. I wanted to be around you. I still want to be around you. I married you. I just don't want you to be my wife only at night. Or when we're in public."

"Then stop treating me like I'm fragile!"

"I don't treat you like you're fragile."

"You do! You're so gentle with me when we're in bed at night, and you'll only make love to me in bed."

"You don't like the way I make love to you?"

"No, I don't like it. I love it. I want more of you, and I don't want you to hold back anymore. It makes me feel like you're bored with me."

"Bored with you?" He turned and grabbed her shoulders. "Are you insane? I want you every moment of the day. But you're pregnant and my wife, and I can't go around taking you against walls and doors and on the kitchen floor."

"Who says?"

He was quiet for a long time. "No one says."

"We're going to be parents in less than seven months. We probably won't be able to be together like that when the baby comes. But we have right now, and we should take full advantage of it."

"You're right." He stood up and took her hand. "Come with me."

"Are you going to take me to bed?"

"Nope. The sunroom."

"But there's so many windows in there."

"I know." He grinned at her and led her away.

Elias glanced over to Cricket, who was lying on a blanket in the sand in front of their house. She was wearing a bikini and starting to show, her belly round and adorable. Her body was changing—her hips were spreading, her breasts growing larger—and as the days passed, his attraction to her also grew. It was a life that they'd created growing inside her, and every time he thought about it, it filled him with pride.

He couldn't resist touching her, and he leaned over and sprinkled kisses on her belly. She grinned and ran her fingers through his curls. Things had gotten a little easier between them in the past couple of weeks. They spent a lot of time together. They had dinner with his siblings at least once a week. They made love whenever the mood struck them, but there was still something there between them that he couldn't identify. A wall that was too high for him to jump over. She was still holding herself back from him.

She didn't trust him. Not to hurt her. Not to turn on her. Not to let her down like so many people had before.

He realized how hard it must have been for her growing up the genius daughter of a billionaire and a trailblazer. There was no one like her in her town. No one she could relate to. No one to be kind to her.

She was expecting him to turn into all those people who had let her down before. And maybe he couldn't blame her for being worried about it. If she hadn't gotten pregnant, he wouldn't have seen her again. He would have walked away, gone on with his life. But he knew now that he never would have completely forgotten about her. He would have wondered what had happened. It probably would have been one of the few things in his life that he had regretted.

So why hadn't he gone after her? What held him back?

No one had ever made him feel the way she did. No one had given him such a rush.

Maybe she had every right not to trust him. He couldn't even trust his own feelings for her. And maybe he had every right to hold a little bit of himself back from her, too. Because as much as he wanted to be with her, he didn't share everything with her. If there was a wall between them, she wasn't the only one who had built it.

He had prided himself on being an open man, but there were certain things he couldn't bring himself to tell her. Like how uncomfortable he was not contributing to the household. The house was paid for, she assured him, the bills automatically deducted from her account. There was no need to change it. She had gone as far as trying to give him half the money for their groceries, but he refused it. He felt like a guest there. Like they were roommates instead of husband and wife. It was her house. Her things. But she was his wife and carrying his child. And he wanted to be a husband and father just like his own father had been. He wanted to take care of his family. But if there was one thing he knew about Cricket, it was that she sure as hell didn't need him.

He wasn't sure what to do about it. He wanted her to be happy here in her beautiful home, especially while she was growing their baby. It might not have made such a difference to him if he were back to work, but he wasn't and he had time to think. And thinking wasn't necessarily a good thing.

"Are you really sure you want to go through with this tonight?" Cricket asked him as he rested his head on her belly.

"Making love to you? You already know the answer to that."

"I'm talking about having my parents over for dinner, you knucklehead." She smiled softly at him.

"Yes, I'm sure. Mostly to show your mother that you haven't bought me a Mercedes."

"You won't let me buy you anything," she pointed out. "Not even ice cream."

"Nope." He wouldn't let her spend a dime when they went out.

"But you bought me a locket." She touched the heart-shaped pendant that rested between her breasts. There was one diamond chip in it to represent their firstborn. She'd cried when he gave it to her. "And my beautiful ring. And those slippers when my feet started to swell in the supermarket the other day."

"I wish I could do more," he said, wanting to say more to her.

She was quiet for a long moment, and he wished he could read the expression on her face, but he was unable to. "You don't have to do anything for me."

"I do. You're going to be giving me the biggest and best present that I will ever have."

She cupped his face and pulled him up so that their lips connected. "You are so incredibly sweet sometimes that I don't know how to handle it."

He knew that she didn't know how to be in an intimate relationship like this. She'd claimed her last boyfriend—whom she'd wanted to marry—was sweet to her, but he wasn't so sure of that. The man sounded more interested in his academic endeavors than he did her.

It was no wonder she didn't realize how desirable she was.

"I have to go inside and start getting dinner ready."

"Stay here." She stroked his cheek with her thumb. "You don't have to cook. We can take my parents out for dinner."

"No. We're entertaining like grown-ups." He sat up and tugged on her hand until she was sitting up. "Come help me cook."

"I might burn the place down."

"That's a risk I'm willing to take. Come inside with me," he urged, not wanting to be away from her just yet.

Cricket stayed with him in the kitchen, watching

him cook at first, asking him dozens of questions. It was why she was so smart. Her unfailing curiosity was why she kept learning. Elias admired that about her. But he wasn't content to have her just sit there and observe him. He wanted her participation. He set her to work, chopping and stirring while he made garlic-and-herb-stuffed pork chops with roasted potatoes and string beans. He knew it would take her mind off her anxiousness. All day he had been trying to keep her calm. She still wasn't on good terms with her mother. He hated that and felt like it was his fault, even though he knew it wasn't.

He was determined to make this evening pleasant for them, to prove to his mother-in-law that he was a good husband for her daughter. He also needed to show her that he was ready to take over as head of trauma when the doctor who was currently in that position retired.

His work was never far from his mind. After Cricket, his desire to return to surgery ruled most of his thoughts. His mother-in-law held his career in her hands and he hated that, but he knew he would have to play by her rules if he wanted to win in the end.

The doorbell rang, and together Cricket and Elias answered it, presenting a united front. Her father, Jerome, greeted them genuinely and warmly. Dr. Lundy was polite but cool as she greeted him and gave her daughter a stiff hug, before she released her and studied her appearance.

"You're starting to show, dear."

"I am." Cricket rubbed her hand over her small belly.

"Can I offer you something to drink? We have pinot noir and riesling," Elias said to them.

"We made appetizers, too. Crostini and jumbo shrimp."

"Did you have this catered? We could have gone out," Dr. Lundy said with a small shake of her head.

"Elias made everything," Cricket told her.

"Cricket helped."

"You can cook?" Dr. Lundy walked toward the side table where they had laid everything out and carefully studied it.

"You know I'm good with a knife," Elias replied. "And I have to be the one who cooks in this marriage. We would be living off cheese and crackers if I didn't."

"I don't cook, either, Bug," Dr. Lundy said, looking at her daughter with affection. "My work was more important."

"Yes, for you it was," Cricket said softly. Dr. Lundy raised a brow in surprise. There were other issues between the two, but right now wasn't the time for them to hash it out.

Elias ushered them all out to the patio that overlooked the ocean. There was a breeze blowing, the air smelled sweet, the sun was just going down. Hideaway Island was truly one of the most beautiful places on earth.

Jerome and Elias did their best to keep the conversation flowing, but it was tough. Cricket was mostly quiet, and Dr. Lundy only interjected when she deemed what they were saying important enough to respond to. It was very different from Elias's family dinners, where everyone laughed and spoke over one another. There was a warmth in the air that was hard to describe.

Had all of Cricket's family dinners been this way—just her and her parents and some stilted conversation? The current tension could have been all Elias's fault, but for some reason, he felt that there was something even deeper going on here.

"What are you working on now?" Dr. Lundy asked her daughter, apparently having had enough of the men taking charge of the conversation.

"I'm still sorting through my research for my next book. I'm due to go back overseas in a couple of weeks to do a little more research and speak to some colleagues who are still conducting a study there."

"What?" Elias focused on Cricket. "You're not going back, right? You've arranged for someone else to do your part."

"No. Of course I'm going back. Why wouldn't I?"

"Because you're almost in your second trimester, and flying to an impoverished, politically unstable, disease-infested part of the world is not a great idea."

"But I made a commitment to speak. My research helps the medical professionals treat those people. It's important."

"Our baby is more important than your research."

Cricket stiffened. "Are you suggesting that I don't know that?"

"I'm not sure what you know. You didn't seem to know that it was the decent thing to inform your husband that you were flying out of the country. You didn't seem to know that something like that would bother me."

"I didn't think it would be an issue. I have been working on this project for the better part of a year. You know how important my work is to me."

"Of course it is, Cricket! It's a huge issue. I don't care about your work. I don't care about other people half a world away. I care about you. We are married. You should have discussed this with me."

"There's nothing to discuss. This trip has been planned for eight months, and I can't back out now. You of all people should be sympathetic to my problem. You're a trauma surgeon. Your only goal is to save people's lives."

"You weren't pregnant eight months ago. You weren't *my* wife eight months ago. You can back out. No one will blame you for wanting to put your child's health first."

"I will not be putting my baby in danger by going over there!"

"The reason you got pregnant is because you were taking medication that you didn't fully understand the effects of. I'm supposed to stand here and be silent and let you take some other drug, or be exposed to some deadly virus, just because you have do-gooder syndrome? And it's not just your baby. It's *our* baby, and if you think I don't get a say in everything that happens to him or her, you're dead wrong."

"Cricket," Dr. Lundy said quietly. "He's right. I can name fifteen medical professionals who would tell you the same thing."

"You're taking his side!"

She nodded once. "Jerome?"

"I'm sorry, Bug. I agree with your mother."

Cricket looked shocked. The betrayal she felt was clear. Elias wanted to feel bad about it, but he just couldn't muster it. The thought of something happening to her made him feel like he was choking.

"I don't want you to go, Cricket," he said as calmly as he could manage. "I want you to call them and cancel."

"I'm not a child." The stubbornness set on her face. "You cannot order me around."

"You're right. You're not a child, but you're carrying my child and I'm your husband, and for the past two months we've been doing things your way, but not on this. You are not alone in this world anymore. You cannot just think about what you want now. You must think about us. You must think about our marriage. We can't have a good one if you're only going to think about yourself."

"I only think about myself? Are you kidding me? My every thought…" She stopped herself, probably realizing that this argument was going to get even more heated in front of her parents. "I need to get out of here." She stood up and left the table.

"Cricket, don't go." He reached for her hand, but she snatched it away.

Soon after, the front door slammed, and he was left alone with her parents. He buried his face in his hands. Their first big fight. He looked up at his in-laws, who both were expressionless.

"I'd bet you two are really wishing that I hadn't married your daughter right now."

"No. That's not what I'm thinking," Dr. Lundy said with a shake of her head. "If you hadn't blown up that way, I would've."

He frowned in confusion, not sure he had heard her correctly. "Excuse me?"

"You were right. We agree with you. What more do you want?"

"She's our only child," Jerome said. "You're her husband, and as much as she doesn't think she needs to be looked after, she does. And that's why she fell for you, because you care for her in a way that no one else ever has."

"I'm crazy about her. I can't even begin to explain it."

"Keep being crazy about her," Jerome said. "You won't have any problems with me as long as you are."

It was late when Cricket returned to the house. Just after 11:00 p.m. Her parents were long gone, the house mostly dark, except for the light over the front door and a lamp in the living room. Elias had left them on for her.

He hadn't waited up. He hadn't come after her. He had only called her twice and when she didn't pick up, he sent her a simple text message.

I'm not asking you to come home yet, even though I want you to. I'm not even asking you to talk, but I need to know you're safe.

She didn't know what kind of danger he thought she would get into on Hideaway Island, but the way he phrased his words took some of the steam out of her righteous anger. She was still mad as hell at him and her parents, but she wasn't mad enough to sleep elsewhere tonight. She had thought about sleeping in the guest room, but why should she be chased out of her bed because of him?

He had no right telling her to cancel her trip. No right to imply that she was selfish. She wasn't doing it for herself. It was no vacation. She was going to go because she'd spent the last three years researching those people. Studying their illnesses. Following their treatments, educating their local governments on how to prevent the spread of disease.

*Was* going to go.

She had called and canceled a few hours ago.

Her child wasn't the reason she was staying home. Now that she knew she was pregnant, she knew how to take precautions. She wasn't going to put the baby in harm's way at all. It was the fact that she had a husband that made her pick up the phone.

*You are not alone in this world anymore. You must think about us. You must think about our marriage.*

That had gotten to her. She wasn't alone anymore. She'd always had her parents, but she had felt so alone for all these years. Now she was married. She had said yes when she didn't have to. She had made this commitment to be not only his partner, but his wife.

He didn't want her to go. And sometimes she felt like she was more the vessel that carried his child than his wife, but he cared about her. He took care of her, and she'd uprooted his life. She should be able to compromise on this, even though nearly everything inside her wanted to rebel.

She stared at his large slumbering body as she got ready for bed. She wasn't sure how he could look so peaceful sleeping when she was a big ball of angry mess.

She was afraid to let her guard down, to let him closer, because she was afraid that he was going to walk away. Every man she had ever gotten close to had walked away from her. For so long she'd thought it was her.

Part of her still thought it was her.

She slid into bed beside him, her body touching his even though it didn't have to. Their bed was huge. She could have had all the space she wanted, but she pressed herself closer to him because she couldn't help it. Bedtime was her favorite part of the day. She loved their lovemaking. She loved his big hard body, the feeling of safety she got whenever she was with him. She was angry. Hours later she was still angry with him, but that didn't stop her from wanting to be with him.

"I'm glad you're home," he said. "I wasn't going to be able to sleep without you next to me."

"Shut up." She removed her nightgown and climbed on top of him. "You're not going to be able to sleep yet."

"Shut up? You never say that."

"You don't know what I say or who I really am."

"I know. But I want to change that. I want to know you." He was being so damn sweet to her. He had been furious with her earlier. His words harsh. His demands clear. He was asserting his possession of her. She never wanted to feel owned, dependent on any man. She didn't need Elias to survive, but she did need him in her life. She needed him to be happy, and she hated that she needed that.

"I'm going to kiss you." She slid her hands along his jaw. "But I don't want you to enjoy it."

"That's going to be hard," he said with a slight grin.

"I'm mad at you. Don't smile."

He nodded as he pulled her face down to his. He was the one to kiss her, softly at first. A peck, and then a lick across her lower lip. But then his tongue swept into her mouth, and her nipples went even tighter. She wanted to control the kiss. She wanted to control their sex tonight, but she always lost all her thoughts whenever he kissed her like this. Her mind had been the only thing she could count on all these years, but he turned it into mush. He made her feel things that she didn't think she was capable of. And that made her angry, too.

She broke the kiss and looked down at him. His eyes were closed, his body completely relaxed. He looked almost as lost as she felt. "I'm supposed to be the one kissing you."

"So kiss me. I like the way your lips feel on my chest."

"Do you?" she asked him.

"Yes, and on my stomach and…lower," he said with a touch of mischievousness.

"Well, I'm never going to kiss you anywhere again. I don't want you to like it."

"Okay." He ran his hands down her back, stopping on her behind to knead her flesh with his fingers. It was more than arousing, and she didn't know if she wanted him to keep going or ease the persistent throbbing between her legs right then.

He had been very gentle with her lately, despite her assurances that she wasn't fragile. She liked when he could barely control himself. She liked when he was shaking with need for her. "Give me your hands."

He looked at her curiously for a moment but did as she asked, and she placed them behind his head.

"You have to keep your hands to yourself tonight."

"But I need to touch you."

"I'm punishing you." She removed his manhood from his underwear and stroked it. He was already hard. He always was whenever their bodies were close together.

He sucked in a deep breath. "Can't you punish me by giving me the silent treatment instead? I want to touch you."

"No." She looked into his eyes as she rose over him and sank down. He was so large and so deep inside her. She relished this feeling, and it made her think about her ex. He had been right. Ultimately she wouldn't have been happy in a relationship with him, because this feeling was important to her. She and Elias were as close as two people could be, and she wanted to be closer.

She squeezed herself around him. He inhaled sharply and let out a low, deep moan. She felt powerful on top of him. With her body alone, she could give him pleasure, and she savored every expression he made, every sound of satisfaction that escaped his lips.

She rose up again and started to ride him slowly, almost letting him completely slip out of her before she plunged back down. She had her hands behind her on his legs, her thighs spread wide before him. She was putting on a show for him. Changing her tempo when he was enjoying himself too much, slapping his hands away when he attempted to touch her.

She had him gritting his teeth. She would have laughed if it hadn't felt so damn good. Every stroke was bringing her closer to climax—she wanted to prolong it as long as possible, but by torturing him she was torturing herself.

"Go faster," he urged her as he grabbed her hips.

"Don't touch me." She reached for his wrist, but he surprised her by rolling her beneath him. He plunged hard inside her, all his control gone. It was what she had wanted. He'd held out for a long time, but he was a strong man. And that's part of the reason she loved him.

Yes, she did love her husband. She didn't know why she was surprised by that. She wasn't sure when it had happened, exactly. Maybe she had always loved him. Maybe she knew the moment they met that she wanted to end up here with him.

He drove into her hard, their skin slapping together. She knew she was making incoherent noises and digging her fingers into his back, but she couldn't help herself. And she broke, a scream escaping her lips. Elias's climax came moments after hers, and for a long time they lay together, a sweaty mass of limbs.

He kissed the side of her neck and then her jaw and cheek before he pressed his lips to hers and gave her a deep, sweet kiss.

"You enjoyed that," she said to him, still breathless.

"Very much so."

"You weren't supposed to."

"I enjoy everything that has to do with you."

"Stop it! I'm trying to be mad at you."

"I missed you," he said quietly. "I will miss you if

you go away, and I'll worry about you and I won't be able to sleep knowing my family is halfway across the world."

A large hard lump sneaked into her throat. "Why didn't you just tell me that before you got all macho and bossy with me?"

"I was mad. Your wife tells you that she's leaving you—you get mad."

"You could have come with me."

"If you're dead set on going I will, just to make sure you stay inside the protective bubble that I'm going to lock you in."

"I'm not going. I called and canceled."

"I thought you weren't going to listen to me."

"I was tempted to tell you to go to hell, but the truth is, I want you to be happy. And I know that you aren't. I don't want this marriage to fall apart, and I know if I can't compromise with you now, in a few years I'm going to look back and hate myself for not doing something so simple."

He kissed her throat and then buried his face there. "You've been afraid we're not going to make it this entire time, haven't you?"

"Yes, haven't you?"

"When people in my family get married, they stay married. I would feel like a total failure if we couldn't make this work."

"Why did you have to go and marry me? It's so much pressure. It's suffocates me."

"I needed to be married to you."

*For the baby*, he didn't say, but she knew that's what he meant.

"I'm not sure how to be your wife. Sometimes I don't read people the right way. You have to let me know if I'm doing something that bothers you. I need you to tell me."

"I will. You have to talk to me, too, Cricket. Don't keep yourself away from me. If we're going to fail at this, we need to go down flaming. With everything out on the table."

"Okay." She nodded.

"What can I do to make you happier?" he asked her as he stroked her cheek.

*Love me.*

She couldn't make herself form the words. They hadn't even known each other for four months yet. It was too soon to expect love. To ask for it.

"I'm not unhappy. But I'm feeling you aren't so happy here. Do you want to go back to Miami?"

"Going back won't change anything. I need to work."

"I would offer to speak to my mother about letting you go back, but I don't think that will help you."

"No." He laughed. "It won't. My brother-in-law told me that the hospitalist at Hideaway Hospital is looking to cut back on his schedule as he prepares for retirement. He wanted to know if I would take over three days a week for him. It's such a small hospital and at most they only have a handful of patients admitted, so he sees patients as a primary care physician, as well."

"What did you say?"

"That I have to speak to my wife about it first."

"Way to make me feel extra bad about not talking to you first about leaving the country."

"That's what I was going for." He grinned at her.

"Take the job. You aren't cleared for surgery yet, right?"

"No."

"I think you'll feel better having something to do. And you get to get away from me."

"That's the only downside to it."

"You're very good." She sought out his lips and kissed him. "We're not fighting anymore."

"Good. Although I kind of like fighting with you."

"Do you?"

"Yeah." He slid his hand onto her breast. "The making up is amazing."

# Chapter 9

Elias studied the boy's foot that he was treating. He had taken the job at the hospital, focusing his mind on medicine. Even if it wasn't the kind of medicine he wanted to practice, it was better than not practicing at all.

The kid had a broken big toe. The nail had split in half. The boy had to be in pain, but he looked more sheepish and worried than anything.

"Mrs. Nieves, would you mind running to the vending machines to get Landon a soda while I fix him up?"

She looked up at him with her eyes full of worry.

"Trust me, it will be better for you if you don't see this. Landon is a tough kid. He'll be fine. But we're understaffed. If you pass out, I'm not sure who will treat you."

"Okay, Dr. Bradley." She kissed her son's forehead a dozen times. "Mommy will be right outside."

"I'm all right, Ma. I swear."

Elias waited until she was out of earshot to speak again. "You want to tell me how you really hurt your foot? Because you didn't just stub your toe."

Landon's eyebrows shot up. "You can tell."

"Of course I can tell. I'm a doctor, and I've been ten before. What did you do?"

"Kicked a microwave."

"You kicked a microwave? Why? Were you mad?"

"Nope. I don't know why I kicked it." He shrugged. "It was big and sitting on the lawn, and sometimes I kick stuff just because."

In ten-year-old boy thinking, it was perfectly logical just to kick stuff because it was there.

"Don't do that again, you knucklehead." Elias grinned at him. "Or else you'll be in here every week."

The boy gave him a cheeky smile. "Maybe twice more before summer ends."

"You like coming to the hospital?"

"You're pretty cool," the boy said. "But I get hurt. So do my brothers. My mother said she would put us up for sale, but no one will take damaged goods."

Elias laughed and patched the boy up. He was still thinking about the encounter when he ended his shift at 3:00 p.m. He came home to find Cricket in the kitchen. She was cooking, which shocked him.

"Hey!" He walked over to her and wrapped his arms around her, settling his hands on her belly. "What's this you're doing?"

"Did you know that there are thousands of short cooking videos posted on social media every day? I went online to look something up, and hours later I emerged with a dozen recipes that even I can handle. It's the most excited I've been in years."

"In years? Really?"

She turned in his arms and kissed him. She tasted sweet, like citrus. He wasn't content with just one kiss and took her mouth in a much longer and deeper kiss.

She sighed when he finished and rested her head on his shoulder. "I should have said that I haven't been this excited over anything that hasn't pertained to you in years."

"That's better."

"How was your day?" she asked him.

"Good. Very good," he answered, surprising himself. Six months ago the thought of being a small-town doctor would have given him hives, but he had been taking on shifts at the hospital for the past couple of weeks, and it wasn't nearly as boring as he expected. He was busy but in a different way, and instead of feeling drained physically and emotionally from complex life-threatening procedures, he got a little charge from interacting with his patients. "I just finished treating a broken toe. Kid kicked a microwave."

"Why?"

"Because he's a ten-year-old boy, and that's what ten-year-old boys do."

"Don't tell me that. I'll be a nervous wreck until our child is fifty."

"Didn't you ever get hurt as a kid? It's normal."

"No. I read. It's hard to get hurt when you spend all of your free time with your nose in a book."

"Didn't you have a horse?"

"Do you think I rode him?" She looked aghast. "I brushed him and petted him and told him that he was special even if he wasn't as beautiful as the other horses."

She made him smile. Every day. When she was around, he couldn't help it. Things had been much better between them. She seemed happy. He was happier. This wasn't the life he wanted, he wasn't doing the job he wanted, but things weren't bad. He could live this life.

When Cricket was happy, the entire world seemed to be brighter.

"Whatever happened to your horse?"

"He's here on the island. Where do you think I went when we had our fight?"

"He's here? And you never told me?"

"I thought I did. He's in the most beautiful stable. It's not far from your brother's house."

"You have to take me to see him."

Her entire face lit up. "You really want to?"

"Of course. I married an heiress. I feel like it's your duty to expose me to fancy crap."

"Let's go right now."

"Right now? I thought you were cooking."

"It's all prepared. All I have to do is pop it in the oven when we get home. It will be ready in a half hour."

"Sounds good. Let's go."

"You're not too tired from work?" She looked at him with a touch of concern.

"No," he answered truthfully. For the first time in his career, he didn't come home exhausted. He came home when it was light, to a warm home and a soft woman. But his hand was getting stronger. The occupational therapist he was seeing on the island worked wonders. Elias had worked so hard to become a trauma surgeon. It wouldn't be much longer now before he was cleared to go back. His single-minded dream had been to be the head of his department, but he was married now. They were going to have a family. He wanted to see his children after school. He wanted to have dinner with them. But it seemed impossible to match his career goals to his family goals.

They still had some time, but he was going to have to think hard and figure out how to make things work out for them.

There weren't many perks to being an heiress. She knew that she could give it all up in an instant. But being able to keep her old, slow horse in this luxurious stable was one of them. The stable had a view of the ocean in the distance. Each horse had a designer stall and the best organic food money could buy. There was a lot of land for the horses to roam freely. It was horse paradise, and her old boy was here. Not because she loved horses or even animals, for that matter, but because as a child, she'd been watching a show on some animal-themed network, and she saw him, abused, nearly half-starved, and she had burst into tears. Her father got on the phone, tracked down the horse and gifted him to her for her fourteenth birthday. Seymour had been here ever since, eating all the food he could get his hooves on.

"This is way nicer than anyplace I have ever lived," Elias said with awe in his voice when they got out of the car.

"It's extravagant, but it's the only thing I treat myself to. I just want Seymour to be happy. He was a rescue. His life hasn't always been this good."

"Seymour." She could hear the grin in his voice. "I like it. I'm assuming he's the chunky gray one grazing over there."

"He's not chunky! He's delightful looking." Seymour looked up at the sound of her voice and came trotting over to the gate from his spot in the field. "There's my boy!" She ran her hand down his long neck, and he nuzzled her.

She climbed over the fence to get closer to him.

"Cricket! What are you doing? You could hurt yourself."

"Relax," she said as she hugged her horse. "I'm fine. My boy is so gentle. He knows he's been saved. He's grateful."

"I'm sure he is. But I don't like you climbing things."

"I guess I won't be going mountain climbing to-morrow. Damn." She looked back at him with a grin. "Seymour, come say hello to your new daddy."

Seymour eyed Elias and then walked a step closer to the gate. Elias eyed Seymour back. It was clear that Elias had never been around such a large animal before, but he calmly walked over to him and extended his hand. "Is it like a dog? Do I let him just smell me?"

"You should always approach every animal with caution," she said to him. "But he's a good boy. Just stroke the bridge of his nose."

"I've never been this close to a horse. When my brother was wooing his wife, he rented horses and took her horseback riding on the beach."

"Romantic." She grinned, thinking about her brother-in-law. It seemed out of character for Carlos, but he loved Virginia so much she knew he would do anything for her.

"Do you want me to do that for you?"

"No. You already gave me the most romantic moment of my life."

"Did I?"

"Yes. You made me a pickle, cheese and mayo sandwich and then made love to me like the contents of my stomach didn't gross you out."

He threw back his head and laughed. He had been so much happier lately. He laughed easier. He was more relaxed. He shared what was on his mind. She was loving the life they had carved out here on the island. She never wanted to leave it. But she knew that as soon as he was cleared to go back to surgery, he would go back. He'd worked too hard not to. Then he would be tired and stressed and she would never see him. It would be like being married to the male version of her mother.

She had avoided surgeons most of her adult life, only to end up madly in love with one.

"My wife was having a craving. It's my job to make sure you always have what you need."

She leaned over the pen and kissed him, feeling that love grow a little deeper. There were so many times she wanted to tell him how much she loved him. But she couldn't. Not yet. She didn't feel safe enough to. Not until she had a sure sign that he loved her, too. It was still far too soon to expect it from him.

"I'm having a craving for frozen custard." She kissed him again. "It would make me very happy if we went to get some."

"Your wish is my command." He looked at her for a long moment. There was genuine affection in his eyes. It made her feel warm all over. The butterflies were still there whenever she looked at him.

The rush. The feeling like the cutest boy in school was paying attention to her.

It was utterly ridiculous. She was a scientist. She had two doctorates. She was nearly thirty! But Elias was gorgeous and strong, and he just made her feel things that she hadn't thought were possible.

"Let's head to the barn and feed Seymour a treat before we head home. I suddenly feel the need to get back there."

He gave her a slow smile, and the look in his eyes turned hot. She loved when he looked at her that way. It meant they probably weren't going to make it to the bedroom.

They began walking back toward the barn a little faster than necessary, Seymour moseying behind them. Neither one of them spoke, but there was heat crackling between them.

Elias was on the outside of the pen and she was inside, but she was glad there was a fence between them, because she knew they wouldn't have even made it back to the barn to feed her horse if there hadn't been.

"Can't you make your horse move any faster?" he asked her as they approached the opening to the building.

"He was built for comfort. Not for speed," she said, grinning. She was still looking at Elias when she heard a shout and the loud pounding of hooves. His horrified expression was the last thing she saw before a big, powerful force slammed into her.

## Chapter 10

Elias's voice was still raw twenty-four hours later. He remembered screaming Cricket's name. He remembered reaching for her as the horse thundered toward her. He remembered seeing her body fly through the air and then go deadly still. He had frozen, rooted to his spot for a few short moments just paralyzed with fear.

*No. No. No.* His mind screamed. *Not her. Don't take her. I can't lose her.*

A panic-stricken teenage girl rushed up to him, and that forced Elias to spring into action. He was a trauma surgeon. He could help her. He would not lose her if he could help her.

He got her stabilized on a board the owners had

in the barn, and a few of the farmhands lifted her into the back of a pickup truck. The horse farm was on a deserted part of the island, and they'd get her to the hospital faster than an ambulance would have.

He treated her once they got back to Hideaway Hospital. Checked her vitals, made sure she was stable. Raised all hell until a helicopter arrived and airlifted her to Miami. Her bones were intact, but she had been hit so hard and there had been so much blood. All because an unruly horse got spooked and ran her way.

The staff at Miami Mercy wouldn't let Elias past the waiting room as they rushed Cricket into surgery. They didn't give a damn who he was or how long he'd worked there. But he knew that they were the best team in the state. That they wouldn't let her die, not because she was the daughter of the chief of surgery, but because they were excellent at their jobs.

He was going stir-crazy waiting for word when a strong hand clamped on to his shoulder. Cricket's father was there. His face tight with worry. The man embraced him hard, and it was what he needed. It was like having his own father hug him. He had been missing his father so much lately, wondering if he was okay with his life choices, with the woman whom he chose to love, to marry.

And through Jerome Warren's tight hug, it was like his own father giving him comfort, promising him everything was going to turn out okay.

Elias knew life would lose its brightness without his sunny wife.

But Cricket did pull through. She was the only one to pull through the ordeal. Their baby didn't make it.

He felt horrible because he hadn't once thought about their baby, only his wife.

He was the one to break the news to her when she woke up and reached down to touch her belly. And it was the most painful moment of his life when he heard the strangled wail she released when the news fully hit her.

Their little family had been shattered. She turned away from him when he reached out to comfort her.

But how could he offer comfort? There were no words. Nothing he could say to make things better. So he settled on holding her hand and not leaving her side until she was released from the hospital a week later.

Things weren't the same between them when they got home.

How could they be?

She'd been so excited about the baby. Excited to be a mother. All her future plans had revolved around the baby. All *their* future plans. And now they seemed to have nothing ahead of them. The house felt empty. Elias had suggested that they stay at his condo in Miami to be closer to her parents, but she wanted to come back to the island, to this house on the water.

He had wanted her to go to bed and rest, but

she sat in the sunroom with the door open and just watched the ocean for days. She sat there from sunup to the moment he physically lifted her out of her seat at night and brought her back to their bedroom.

It was nearly a month later when he realized that he needed to do something more to get his wife back to living.

Cricket felt numb. It was the only way to describe what was going on with her. She was absolutely numb. She was wrecked, she knew, but she couldn't describe the feeling as sadness. She was too far beyond that, and now she felt nothing. Not hunger or thirst or pain or anything. She was pretty sure she would have wasted away if it weren't for Elias. He made sure her body healed correctly after surgery. He fed her. He put her to bed. He even bathed her, filling their huge bathtub with hot soapy water and climbing in it with her. He just held her while the water gently lapped over her. His strong chest keeping her upright when she might otherwise have sunk in.

There was one emotion that was still lurking beneath, and it was love. If she hadn't known that she was in love with him before, she knew now. Head over heels in love. Crazy in love, but now she had nothing to offer him.

The baby was the only reason he had married her. It was a boy. They had learned after she miscarried. That child was their only connection, and now he was gone. Elias would be gone, too. Eventually. He was too good a man to leave her right now when she was at her lowest, but he would eventually go and live the life he had wanted before she had gotten pregnant.

About three and a half weeks afterward, she knew she could no longer continue to walk around like a zombie. She got herself up one morning. She dressed herself and combed her hair and made a large pot of coffee, and instead of sitting in the sunroom, she forced herself to leave the house and walk on the beach.

She couldn't remember the last time she had been out of the house. It was probably to head to the doctor for a checkup. It was nice to be outside in the cool morning air. The breeze whipped her curls around, feeling good against her skin. She stood at the edge of the water, the waves covering her feet before they retreated.

She heard her name being called and heavy footsteps behind her. Fear zigzagged through her, and for a moment she was unclear why. She didn't remember the horse running toward her. She only remembered waking up in the hospital to Elias's twisted face telling her that she wasn't going to be a mommy anymore. But she did remember the noise of the hooves beating the ground and Elias's voice screaming out her name.

This time he grabbed her shoulders and pulled her into him. Crushing her against him so tightly it hurt.

"What's the matter, baby?" she asked him.

"I didn't know where you were." He pulled away from her slightly and looked into her eyes. The worry was clear in them, and so was the relief. "You scared me! You aren't allowed to scare me anymore. Promise me you won't."

He was afraid she was going to hurt herself. The thought horrified her. She would never do that to herself, to him. But he didn't know that, because for the past month she'd ceased to be a person.

"I'm sorry." She closed the gap between them and smoothed her hand down his strong back. "I just wanted to go for a walk."

"Let me walk with you."

"Aren't you sick of me?"

"No! I'm sick at the thought of being without you."

Her eyes went wide at his statement, and suddenly the numbness that was a constant companion washed away.

She knew he had been hurt, too, by the loss of their child, but he had also been worried about losing her, which was something she hadn't cared so much about the past month.

She stood on her tiptoes and leaned in to kiss him softly. But he didn't want just a soft kiss. He cupped her cheeks and kissed her harder. It was the first time they had kissed like this since the day of her accident.

"Let me take you out to breakfast," she said when he broke the kiss.

"Are you sure you're up for that?"

"As long as you are with me."

## Chapter 11

Two days later Cricket sat in the living room with her parents, a mug of steaming tea in her hands. Her mother had been to the island three times in the past month, which was a lot considering her work schedule. Her father had come twice a week without fail.

They had been so worried about her, and every other time that they had visited, she had been only vaguely aware of their presence. Now she was fully engaged, but it was exhausting. She was no longer numb, but the heaviness was still there and today it was taking everything in her power not to crawl back into bed.

She looked over to Elias, who was sitting in an overstuffed armchair, too far away from her to touch.

She wanted to be sitting next to him, to lean against him. She could have gotten up from her seat to be with him, but she felt that she was leaning on him too much, that it was time to prop herself up. She'd been totally independent before him. She would need to be after him, too.

"What are your plans now, sweetheart?" her mother asked her.

Cricket wasn't sure why the question took her off guard, but it did. "Um… I—I guess I'll go back to writing my book. I shouldn't keep my publisher waiting."

"Maybe you should go back to teaching. There are quite a few excellent universities in Miami, and you'll have to settle there anyway, once Elias goes back to surgery in two weeks."

"In two weeks?" She looked over to him.

He nodded. "I was going to wait until we were alone to talk about it." He gave her mother a pointed look. "I've been cleared. The result of my latest scan came back this morning."

"When did you go to the doctor?"

"The day Ava and Derek came to be with you. I told you I was going," he said gently.

She had heard him tell her that, but she hadn't been listening. "That's right. You did. I'm happy for you," she said, but her voice didn't really convey it. She didn't want to go back to Miami. She didn't want him working sixteen-hour days. She didn't want him to be so driven, like her mother was, but she had no right to feel that way. She was being selfish, wanting to keep him all to herself when she knew that all he wanted to do was reach the top.

"We can talk about this more later," he said to her.

"Why wait?" Dr. Lundy said. "We're here. We can help you two figure things out."

"I think we can figure our lives out for ourselves, Doctor. But thank you." Elias's voice was tight. Her mother had been offering what she thought was helpful advice the entire time she had been there. It was starting to become grating.

"You are married to my daughter, and you do work for me. I think I have a large role in your lives. Maybe you should look at this loss as a blessing in disguise. Now everything won't happen so quickly. You can take time to evaluate what you both really want out of life and your marriage, and you won't have to rush into anything."

"I used to think your ability to separate your feelings from your thoughts made you an excellent surgeon," Elias said, his voice deadly low. "But now I just think you are the most insensitive person on the planet."

Her mother's eyes widened with surprise. She clearly had no idea what he was talking about, how her words sliced through them.

"How can I be insensitive? You now have one less thing to worry about."

"One less thing!" he roared. "That one less thing was the thing we wanted above all else, and if you can't pull your head out of your behind long enough to see that, then we don't need you here. Our loss is not a blessing! Our lives are not lived to please your stupid, impossibly high standards."

"Excuse me?"

"Get out. You can't even see that you are upsetting your daughter. Just go."

"Surely you aren't kicking me out of the house my husband and I purchased for our daughter. As far as I'm concerned, *you* are the guest here."

"You're right. This isn't my home, and it never will be."

He walked out of the room.

"Frances!" Jerome looked furious. "Sometimes you go too far. This isn't your hospital. Elias is no longer just your employee. He's our son-in-law, and if you can't see that he's clearly in love with our daughter, maybe you should get your vision checked."

Cricket sat there reeling. She didn't know whether to go after her husband or yell at her mother. "You wished this on me, didn't you?"

Dr. Lundy looked stricken. "Why would you say such a thing?"

"Why can't you be happy for me when I'm happy and grieve with me when I'm sad? I wanted that baby more than I've ever wanted anything in my life, and you're acting relieved that it's not happening."

"It's not that I—"

Elias came back from the bedroom with a large

suitcase in his hand. Cricket's eyes filled with tears. He was walking out.

How could she blame him?

This wasn't his house, or his dream or his idea of a good life. And her mother had forced his hand. She would walk out, too, just to make the same point.

"Come on, Cricket." He extended his hand to her, uncertainty in his eyes. Without thinking, she stood and took it.

"Cricket..." Her father stood up. "Don't go. This is your home. Both your home. Please, stay."

"I'm sorry, Daddy, but I have to go."

"Cricket," her mother said as she stood. "You can't really be serious about leaving."

"I am. I'm choosing my husband. You can keep the house."

Elias looked over to his wife, who was dozing beside him on Carlos's private plane. It was one of the perks of having a brother who was one of the wealthiest athletes in the world.

Cricket had never asked where they were going. There was no uncertainty in her eyes when he'd extended his hand to her and asked her to come. She trusted him, and it made him love her even more. She could have been upset with him—maybe she should have been upset with him for yelling at her mother and ordering the woman out. But Cricket was with him all the way, and that made him feel better than he had in a very long time.

He kissed the side of her face, unable to help himself. She opened her eyes and looked up at him.

"I'm an heiress, but not one person in my family owns a private plane."

"My brother isn't into cars or shoes or bling. Before he bought his house on the island, he was living in the same one-bedroom condo he had since he was a rookie. The other players started to tease him for being cheap, so he bought a plane to show them. I think he wasn't allowed into the special superrich athlete club until he bought one."

"I knew baseball players made a lot of money, but I didn't know that they made that much."

"My brother invests in things right before they explode into huge businesses. He's gotten me into some of them."

"Things like what?"

"Dating apps. Car services. Health food stores. Even if I never worked as a surgeon, I can take care of you. You can have whatever you want."

"I don't want anything."

"I know, but I have so much I want to give to you."

"You've given me so much already. I feel selfish. Sometimes I wish you weren't so sweet to me."

*I love you.* He didn't say the words. He couldn't bring himself to in that moment. "You haven't asked me where we were going."

"It doesn't matter. I think I needed to get away."

"We're going to Costa Rica."

"To meet your mother?"

"And my grandmother and aunts." They had video chatted a dozen times or so since they had been married, but his mother couldn't leave Costa Rica because of her mother's poor health. His grandmother was going to be ninety-seven this year. He understood why she couldn't leave her.

"Are we staying with them?"

"No. I never got to take you on a honeymoon. I figured we could take care of that while we're there."

"Elias." Cricket surveyed the scene from their house, and it took her breath away. She had been breathless a lot today. She had spent so much of her time in poor, underdeveloped countries the past ten years that she had forgotten how truly gorgeous the world could be. Hideaway Island was beautiful and tropical, but there was a small-town, homey feeling whenever she stepped foot on it, but here in Costa Rica… She couldn't even describe what she was seeing. She knew they were at a resort. There'd been a lobby with a check-in desk. They had passed a spa, some pools and a few restaurants, but they kept traveling through all of that until they got to a three-story house that seemed to stand alone on a beach. The entire spacious top floor was theirs. Their bedroom led out to a deck that wrapped around the entire unit. There was a gorgeous tiled half-moon-shaped hot tub there overlooking the ocean. But it wasn't just ocean in their view. There was thick lush forest surrounding them and sounds of wildlife that were soothing and exciting at the same time.

"You like it here?" He came up behind her and kissed her shoulder.

"No, I don't like it here." She turned to face him with a slight smile. "I could die here. Right here on this balcony. In fact, bury me in the hot tub. It's incredible."

He looked into her eyes for a long moment. "I missed your smile."

"I'm sorry." She looped her arms around him and leaned against him.

"Why are you apologizing to me?"

"I'm not sure. I just feel the need to."

"I think you should rest. We are going to have the biggest dinner that two people have ever had, and tomorrow you're going to meet the rest of my family. You're going to need your energy for that."

She nodded. "Do you mind if we get in the hot tub first?"

He grinned at her. "I was hoping you'd ask me that."

## Chapter 12

"Your home is beautiful, Mrs. Bradley," Cricket said in a quiet voice.

"Don't call me Mrs. Bradley! You are family now!" Elias's mother, Nilda, wrapped her into a big warm hug. "And thank you. It's very hard to please five women, but Carlos seemed to know that this was the right amount of space for us. I could go two days without seeing any of my sisters if I wanted to—and I often do."

"Ha!" Elias's aunt Arsenia laughed. "You talk more than any of us. We hide downstairs just to get away from your mouth."

A bunch of good-natured bickering followed that, which was typical of any get-together with his mother and her sisters. Elias often wished his mother lived closer to him and his siblings, but he could tell she was happier here. After his father died, she'd been lost without her husband. Being on Hideaway Island, where they had spent family vacations, made her feel empty, but her sisters made her full. There was no space for sadness here. And that's why Elias had thought it would be a good thing for him and Cricket to visit.

They'd had a nice day, a ridiculously huge lunch and a trip to the beach, and now his aunts had whisked Cricket away to go shopping in the nearest village. Elias chose to stay at the house with his mother, who had stayed behind to be with his resting grandmother.

"Abuela looks good," he said to her.

"Yes." She smiled. "She has been so excited to have you here. She wishes you would come around more."

"I know. My work kept me away."

"Your work." She rolled her eyes. "I know most mothers would be thrilled with a doctor and a hugely famous professional athlete for sons, but I would much rather you lived with me for the rest of your lives so I can take care of you."

"Pop taught us to be men, to work hard, to take care of our families."

"He taught you well." She nodded. "You really do take good care of your wife."

"What do you think about me being married?

You didn't react the way I thought you would when I told you."

"You thought I would scream and fuss and carry on?" She shrugged. "I wanted to. If your brother or sisters had gotten married like that, I would have. But I knew for you, my workaholic son, to do something so completely nuts must have meant that the girl was special. You love her very much."

"I do."

"You're both very sad."

"No one wanted to be a mother more than Cricket."

"What about you? Did you want to be a father?"

"Of course I did. I still do. But I didn't think about the baby once the accident happened. For weeks I kept seeing the horse slam into her, her body flying as if she weighed nothing. And then she was so still on the ground. I thought she was gone. She didn't respond to her name. She wouldn't move. But then she did. She opened her eyes and said my name, and I realized that I wouldn't be able to take it if I never heard her say my name again. There isn't one big thing that makes me love her. But there are a thousand little indescribable things."

"And you hate that she is so sad."

He nodded. "It's been five weeks. I can't expect her to snap out of it. It's too soon to tell her that I want to try again."

"You want to try again?" She looked surprised. "I had the feeling that this pregnancy was unplanned."

"It was, but that doesn't mean I wasn't happy

about it. I've been making a crib. Ava's husband has been helping me. I was so excited to meet my son, but I still want that chance. I want to see Cricket be a mother. She has so much love to give."

"Have you spoken to her about this?"

"No. We haven't spoken about anything. There were a few weeks when I couldn't reach her at all. Now I'm starting to get little pieces of her back, and I don't want them to vanish again."

"But you can't go around with things unsaid just because you're afraid of what might happen. You are both going through this. You need to go through it together. It's the only way you'll have a strong marriage."

Elias agreed. He just didn't know how to bring it up to Cricket.

Cricket didn't know when they had gotten to the point in their relationship where they could just be quiet and content in each other's company, but they were there. She felt completely comfortable with him. She felt safe. She had been a living, breathing zombie the past five weeks, but Elias had been her constant. He was the first person she saw when she woke up in the hospital. He had raised hell a few times when he thought she wasn't getting treated fast enough. He was her protector, even going to battle with her mother. She wondered why he was so good. So motivated to be that way.

She could attribute it to his mother. To their strong

family bond. He'd been raised to think that men just acted that way. But she wondered if he was tired of it, if sometimes he just wanted to be catered to.

She wanted to take care of his needs, but it was hard to do when he was so self-sufficient.

She picked up his no-longer-injured hand and kissed his palm a few times. He put down his e-reader and gave her a soft smile. "Have I ever told you that I like it when you do that?"

"Kiss your hand?"

"Kiss me in general. You kiss me a lot. When you wake up. When you leave a room. When I hand you something."

"Does it bother you?"

"No! I just told you that I like it."

"You are the most beautiful man that I have ever seen. You give me butterflies, sir. And I can't believe that you are married to me."

"You're a nerd." He pulled her closer, lifting her with his strong arms until she was half on top of him. He ran his hand up the back of her thigh, his fingers toying with the hem of her dress. She felt a powerful surge of lust strike her. She remembered the day of the accident. They'd been rushing back to the barn so they could go home and get in bed. But they never made it there.

They hadn't been together in over a month. They had been in Costa Rica for three days. They had been naked in the hot tub together. They had slept close together in bed, but he never attempted a thing. She had never felt that kind of hurt before. Recovering physically and mentally from her accident. But her body felt all better now, and she knew he had needs, that he was a man who enjoyed sex and it was her duty as a wife to provide him with it. It was also her joy to give her body to him. She never felt better than when she was in his arms.

"You are also the sexiest woman that I have ever met, and I get great satisfaction just being in your presence."

"Stop being so damn sweet to me." She pulled his lower lip between her teeth and gave it a soft bite before she swept her tongue across it.

"Don't start with me," he growled, lust heavy in his voice. "I want to talk to you."

"You want to talk? Now?"

"Yes. I've been meaning to. I don't think we can go on unless we have this conversation."

She sat up and looked into his eyes, which had gone completely serious. "What do you want to talk about?"

"The baby."

"No." She shut her eyes, feeling the tears so close to the edge. "I can't. I don't want to."

"We have to talk about it. *I* need to talk about it."

"But why? It's over. I was pregnant, and now I'm not."

"It's not over. He was my son, and I wanted to meet him. And I think about him sometimes and what it would be like to see him born and who he would have looked like and what he might have become. And sometimes I think I'm crazy, because how could I love someone so much that I've never even laid eyes on? That I never will lay eyes on? But it was the possibility of what he could have become. It's the thought of seeing you loving him. I feel robbed of the greatest opportunity, and if I feel that way, I know you must feel that way, too. To an even greater extent."

"Of course I do! I was just starting to feel him move. Did I tell you that?" She swiped at the tears on her face. They were coming out so quickly that she was blinded. "I was growing this gift inside me. This gift for you. This gift for the world, and in two seconds it was gone and I blame myself for losing it. For screwing up the most amazing thing I have ever done."

"What!" He shook his head. "You blame yourself? What did you do wrong? It was a freak accident that could have killed you."

"Maybe I could have prevented it. What if I didn't take you to the barn that night? What if I jumped out of the way? What if I fought a little harder to keep the baby?"

"Stop it, damn it! There are no what-ifs. You could not have changed what happened. There is nothing that either of us could have done to change the outcome."

"But I want to change what happened. I wanted to give you a baby. Do you know my favorite part of being pregnant was having you touch my belly? I loved it when you pressed your lips to it and talked to him. That was the one thing I could give you, and now it's gone."

"No, Cricket." She was shocked to see tears well in Elias's eyes. "That was not the one thing you could give me. We can have more babies, but if I lost you that day, I don't know what I would have done. There will never be another you. I will never have another wife."

She was waiting for him to say *like you*. But it never came. Of course he would have another wife if something happened to her. He was a beautiful man inside and out. Any woman would want to be with him.

Even now, he could have anyone else he wanted. Now that the baby was gone, it really hammered home that she wasn't the wife he would have chosen. Their child had bonded them together, and now that child was gone. What was left for them? What was it that would keep them together now?

"I feel so terrible."

"I know." He cupped her face in his hands. "But we can be happy again. I want to see you happy again." He kissed her, his eyes closing, his hands pulling her closer.

She wanted what he wanted. To be happy. Being with him made her happy. But she could never be sure if she was enough to make him happy.

"I need you," she whispered to him as she reached for his shirt. "Please."

"Are you sure you're ready?"

She unbuttoned his shorts and slipped her hand inside, stroking his already-hard manhood. "Undress me."

The lust in his eyes made her wet immediately. She was wearing a simple halter dress that he had packed for her. He had brought all her favorite clothes. He'd even packed the scented lotion she liked. He knew her so well. Better than the man she'd spent five years with, better than her own parents. It was one of the thousand reasons she loved him.

She straddled him. He pulled the tie on her halter, tugging down the bodice as he crushed his mouth to hers. He was a master at undressing her. His nimble fingers unclasped her bra. His hands reached for her breasts, cupping them, running his thumbs over her too-sensitive nipples. She gasped at the sensation, and he pulled his lips from hers and looked into her eyes as he took one of her breasts into his mouth and suckled.

She couldn't stop the moan that escaped her lips. She grasped him with one hand as she pulled her underwear to the side.

"Wait," he said to her as she slid down on him. "I haven't made love to you in a month. Let me at least take you to bed." He grunted as she rose up and slid down on him again. "Let me take my time," he said through gritted teeth. "Let me go slow."

"It's too late. Later. You can go as slow as you want later. I need this from you right now."

# Chapter 13

"Wake up." Elias felt Cricket's lips kiss their way up his throat the next evening. They hadn't made it out of their rental at all that day. They'd barely made it out of bed. They had missed each other, missed being together like they had been. But it was different now. He didn't think it could be more intense than it was before, but in a way it was.

He was glad they'd talked, glad he understood how she was feeling a little more than before. She had always put so much pressure on herself. She lived up to impossible standards, and he blamed her mother, who had conditioned her to never feel that anything she did was right.

He wouldn't allow that to happen anymore. That's

why he had taken her away from there. Neither one of them needed that right now. They needed to heal without someone rooting against them.

"I'm awake." He wrapped his arms around her, pulling her on top of him. He loved her body, the way her large, soft breasts felt pressed against him. "Did you miss me?" He captured her mouth in a long kiss. "It's your fault I passed out. I haven't worked so hard in years."

"Don't kiss me like that," she said, sighing.

"Why?" He ran his hand up her back. She was clad only in her underwear, and in his opinion that was far too many clothes. He unclasped her bra.

"Hey!"

"What? We're on our honeymoon. The dress code is naked, and you started this."

"We've had more sex in the past twenty-four hours than most normal people should."

"Neither one of us is normal, love. And if you don't want to have sex with me, you should probably keep your lips off my throat."

"I didn't say I didn't want to have sex with you. I always want to have sex with you."

"Good." He rolled her onto her back and slipped off her panties. "Why are we still talking?"

He pushed inside her, finding her completely ready to be loved. He kept his eyes open so he could look down at her as he made love to her. He loved the way she looked back at him—there was love in her eyes. Neither one of them had said the exact words, but maybe they didn't need to be said. They had been through so much in such a short amount of time. How could there not be love between them?

He lowered his head to kiss her as he pumped inside her. She never was one to sit back and let him make love to her. She was always an active participant. She always made his lust spike uncontrollably. She wrapped her legs around him. Squeezed herself around his manhood, scraped her nails down his back. He could barely hold on, but she seemed to like him that way, to the point where he was too far gone.

Lucky for him, she came quickly.

He climaxed with her and collapsed on top of her, a happy, exhausted, sweaty mess.

"That was good," she said, patting his back.

"You always say that."

"I always mean it." She grinned at him, and he felt the strong urge to kiss her again, so he did. "Don't start again. We're going to be late."

"For what? Did you make dinner reservations?"

"No. We're going on a private night tour of the nature reserve."

"Are we?"

"Yes. While you were napping, I went to the boutique and bought all the gear we need."

He raised an eyebrow. "What kind of gear would that be?"

"Nothing heavy-duty, just rain gear and long pants. Hiking boots. A waterproof camera. Bug spray."

"How much did you spend?"

"A small fortune, but nothing is too good for my husband."

"Are you sure you're up to a hike in the woods?"

"Yes. It will be a light activity compared to all the sex." She stroked her thumb across his cheek. "You don't want to go?"

"I do."

"Good, because I was going to guilt you into it. Now get off me. We've got to get out of here."

A half hour later, they were in the middle of the rain forest along with their guide, wearing LED lights on their heads. He had been surprised to see how into it Cricket was. She was an academic. She had spent most of their marriage with her head in a book, but he remembered that right before they met she had spent months roughing it in developing nations, surrounded by poverty and infectious diseases. She was brave, his little wife. She went over the tiny suspension bridges without an ounce of fear, looking down at the forest floor and asking a thousand questions. They saw owls, lizards and frogs on their journey. The only thing Cricket balked at was the large tarantula they spotted. Even Elias was uneasy about that one, but she had buried her head in his back and wrapped her arms around his waist and asked him to guide her as far away from it as possible.

When their tour was over, they lingered outside, slowly heading toward their rental. There was a warm breeze blowing, the sky was clear and dark, and they could see every star in the sky. They stopped at the hot springs, which during the day were full of people bathing. They were empty now. Quiet. The only sounds came from the rushing waterfall and the wildlife singing in the distance. This was paradise. Elias never wanted to leave it.

"Let's get in," she said, looking up at him.

"Do you have your bathing suit?"

"Nope." She gave him a cheeky smile as she set down her bag and pulled off her top. "Do you think that's going to stop me?"

"Cricket." One hot surge of lust hit him square in the pants. He'd never thought it would be possible for one woman to turn him on so much.

"Elias." Her grinned widened. "Take your pants off. You know you want to."

"We can't have sex out here," he said to her as she stripped off the rest of her clothing.

"I know. I'm planning to make you suffer."

He was already suffering. It was painful to feel this kind of need. He took off his clothing, placing it on top of hers and following her into the hot springs. The hot tub was nothing in comparison to this. The water felt different, cleaner, the air was thick and tropical, the surroundings were too beautiful for words, and he was with a woman who had a naughty side that he was growing fonder of by the moment.

"Tell me some nerdy facts about these hot springs," he said to his wife.

"They are heated by a volcano," she started. "This

one is about one hundred and two degrees, give or take a few. Because of the natural minerals, the water is supposed to leave your skin moisturized and refreshed."

He grinned at her. It never ceased to amaze him that someone so smart could look so damn mouthwateringly sexy. She was a pinup. She had the kind of body that was meant to be covered in oil and draped over a sports car, but she was also brainy. And somehow he'd had the good fortune to be placed in her path. "Come here." He sat on a man-made rock bench that was located just in front of a small waterfall. She obeyed his request, coming to sit beside him instead of on his lap like he wanted.

"You're too far away from me."

"I know. I'm afraid to touch you."

"You should never be afraid of that. Come here." He grabbed her hand and pulled her into his arms. Their wet bodies slid against each other, arousing him more.

"We cannot fool around in here. I don't care how clothing optional this resort is."

"Clothing optional? I didn't know that. I just thought you were being naughty."

"I am! My mother would have a heart attack if she knew what we were up to."

"Don't worry about her." He kissed her shoulder.

"I'm not sure how you two are going to get along when you go back to work."

"I'm not going back to work for her. I sent in my resignation three days ago."

"What?" Her eyes went wide. "You love that job."

"Yes, but I can do it anywhere. What I can't do is work for your mother. Especially after what went down between us. She doesn't have a say in our lives. You and I are the ones who decide."

She looped her arms around his neck and held on to him tightly. "You don't have to do this. I'm sure you can work things out with my mother. She didn't mean to hurt us."

"But I saw the look in your eyes when she said those words. When we get back home, I'm going to apply at other hospitals in Miami, and if it's okay with you, I'm going to start looking outside south Florida. I've got contacts all over, including at the Davis Clinic. One of my former teachers is a chief of surgery there."

"That's the best hospital in the country."

"I wouldn't be applying for trauma. Thoracic surgery would become my specialty again. My hours would be steadier. More routine scheduled procedures."

Cricket made a soft noise but didn't say anything else. They were just speaking in what-ifs, but if he got a job there they would have to move to the middle of the country, away from both of their families. It was a lot to ask of her, but they could make their own family, and they could always visit Hideaway Island.

"I won't apply if you don't want me to."

"Of course you have to apply. If you have the chance to work at the best hospital in the country, you should go. I have been there before to work with their microbiologist in their infectious disease clinic. I've never met a group of more brilliant scientists."

"That's good to hear. We don't have to make any decisions yet. I think we should wait until we find out for sure if you're pregnant again."

"Pregnant again?" She looked startled for a moment.

"The doctor did say we shouldn't have a problem getting pregnant again, right?"

"She said I should be fine."

"I think we should wait till we get back to the States before we take a test. But we can get one here, too. Although I'm not sure if we can get an early-response test here."

"How long are we staying here?"

"As long as you want, but I reserved three weeks."

She kissed his shoulder a half-dozen times. "I want to stay here with you the entire three weeks, but I have something to tell you."

"What is it?"

"I'm not pregnant."

"I think it's too soon to know for sure, but we're fertile. You might be."

"No, I really mean that I'm not pregnant. I can't be. I had the doctor give me a shot of Depo-Provera."

"That's a long-lasting shot. The effects can last longer than six months."

"I know. I didn't think you would want to try again so soon. The doctor wanted me to wait eight weeks before trying to get pregnant again, and this just seemed like the right thing to do."

"You know how much I want to be a father."

"You will be a father." She pressed her lips to his mouth. "You will have all the happiness you want, because it's what you deserve."

Even though his wife was pressed against him and she was saying the right words, Elias felt uneasy. He felt like she was disconnecting herself from his life once again.

Cricket had thought that Hideaway Island was her happy place. The place where no pain could reach her and all her memories would be happy ones. But real life had infiltrated her peaceful sanctuary there. She had lost her baby there. Gotten into the biggest fight she had ever had with her parents there. But she had also met Elias there. She'd made love for the first time there. She had truly fallen in love on that little island, and having so much joy and so much pain connected to one place taught her a valuable lesson. Life can reach you wherever you hide.

They were in paradise, she and Elias. It had been nearly three weeks full of deep, delicious lovemaking and fantastic food. She got to be encased in the love of Elias's extended family. She got the chance to be spoiled by his mother. They had all been so kind to her, and part of her never wanted to go back

to the States. They could make a life here in paradise, she thought. They could wake up to the sounds
of wildlife and look out the window and see nothing
but unspoiled rain forests and ocean water so clear
and blue that it looked unreal. Elias could easily get
a job here, a job with even more prestige than he had
back at home. She could spend her days writing and
doing research in the medical field at a university.
They could have children here and raise them in a
different culture.

It could be a wonderful life, and Cricket knew
that all she had to do was say the word to Elias, and
he would make it all happen. He wanted her to be
happy, no matter the cost to himself, and that's why
she loved him so much. And that's why she knew
she couldn't stay there forever, because it wasn't the
life he had dreamed for himself. They had unfinished business back on Hideaway Island. And even
though this place was pretty much perfect, she still
missed being home. She had spoken a few times
to her father, who was truly distraught with how
things had gone down before they left. He told her
that her mother was upset, but her pride and strong
will wouldn't allow her to apologize. Cricket didn't
need an apology, but Elias did. He was the one who
had sacrificed so much. She needed to find a way to
give him as much as he had given her.

She looked over to him. They were lying on the
beach at twilight, their favorite time of day. It was
completely empty. There was a lovely warm breeze

blowing and the sound of waves lapping the shore. Elias was dozing next to her on his lounge chair, a panama hat draped over his face. She had bought it for him. She thought he looked unbearably sexy at the moment, wearing swim trunks and a short-sleeved blue button-up shirt open to reveal his hard chest, which she had a hard time not running her fingers over.

She got up from her chair and plucked the hat off his face, only because she felt the desperate urge to kiss him in that moment.

She should have known he wouldn't let her get away with just one kiss to the cheek. He pulled her down on the chair, shifting his body so that they both could lie there together. He ran his hand over her bottom. At his request she had purchased a white bikini. It was even sexier than the one she had worn that day she spent with his family. She had felt horribly self-conscious in it. But he kept looking at her, touching her. He enjoyed her body. She had spent so long with a man who was uninterested and unable to be sexual—being married to a man who was the opposite of that was making her feel alive in a way she hadn't thought possible.

"You didn't think I was going to let you walk away from me, did you?"

"I just wanted to give you a little kiss."

"You know I can't take the way you look in this bathing suit." He slid his hand to her back and un-hooked the top of her bikini. Her breasts came free and he touched them, smoothing his large, skilled hands over them.

"You need to stop that," she moaned.

"Why?"

"We can't do this here."

"Why not? No one is around. We're all the way at the end of the beach."

"Someone could easily walk up."

"Yes." He kissed her shoulder. "But I doubt they will."

"I don't think this chair will hold up to our love-making."

"That, I'll have to agree with." He turned her so that most of her back was touching the chair and he was half atop her, and then his hand wandered to her bikini bottoms, inside to her lower lips. He groaned when he felt her there. "So soft. So wet."

She felt slightly embarrassed by his words, but they caused her to become even more aroused. "You do this to me. Only you could ever do this to me."

"You make me crazy," he said before he took her mouth. "I can no longer think straight when I'm near you."

He slipped his fingers inside her, stroking her slowly but firmly. She knew she should just lie back and enjoy him, but she was unable to be passive when she was with him. She needed to give back to him. She reached inside his swim trunks and took his hardness in her hand. He hissed in pleasure. She worked fast, knowing she was only moments away from explosion herself.

He kept kissing her, those long, deep, breath-stealing kisses that made her feel otherworldly.

Orgasm struck, and she cried into his mouth. He spilled himself in her hand and kissed her one last time before he got up and led her into the warm ocean water. She was topless, but on this resort clothing was optional. She wouldn't have felt comfortable enough to do that if there were anyone else there.

The ocean water was incredibly warm, the waves gentle. Cricket wrapped her body around her husband's, and they just floated together.

"It's going to be hard to leave this place," she said as she kissed his shoulder.

"We can stay longer if you want. There's nothing pressing to get back to."

"Except life. You have a career that I know you must be missing."

"You're more important to me."

"I'm surprised no one married you before I got the chance. You are a very good husband. Have I told you that? You're a better man than I ever could have wished for."

"There was no one that I wanted to marry before you came along."

She'd gotten pregnant. That's why he married her, and she couldn't forget that. She wouldn't have seen him again if she hadn't. "Are you going to apply for that out-of-state job when we get back?"

"Unless you don't want me to."

"I want what you want. It's a simple as that."

"I want to buy the house from your father."

"What?"

"I have a lot of money saved. I've made good investments. My salary is high enough to support us both. I could buy the house from him."

"No, I don't want you to do that."

"Then we can buy a new house on the island together. I know you love your house, but if we buy a new house, we could make it our own. I like the house, but I feel like it's your house."

"It's not my house. It doesn't feel like home without you there. I'm sorry if I've made you feel like a guest there."

"You haven't."

"My father won't take your money. I know he won't. That was his gift to me when I finished my second PhD."

"I won't feel like it's my home unless I have paid something for it. I think he'll understand where I'm coming from if I sit down and have a conversation with him."

"He likes you. I feel like you want to do this to prove something to my mother. You don't need her approval."

"I hurt my hand and then I met you and then we were going to have a baby and then we lost the baby, and everything in my life felt so out of control. I haven't felt that way since my father died. I can control how I treat you. The work I do. How we live. The kind of father I will be."

"You still wish I was pregnant, don't you?"

"Of course I do. Don't you? I want to make a family with you."

"How many kids do you want? We never discussed it. We got married so quickly. We didn't know each other. Sometimes I think we still don't know each other."

"I know you. I know that your favorite color is marigold yellow. And that you love to spend rainy days in bed. Your favorite food is ice cream, and you'd rather eat that than real food. I know that bugs scare you and having fresh flowers in the house makes you happy. I know you want a simple life. And to answer your question, I want a lot of kids, but I'll settle for as many as you want to give me as long as it's more than one."

Life wouldn't be so simple if he went back to being a surgeon in one of the best hospitals in the world. He would work all the time. He would miss out on large parts of their children's lives. He would try to be there. He would love them, but he wouldn't be able to leave his patients behind because his work was too important. And she wouldn't be able to travel the world and work in less-than-safe places, because she knew that she couldn't risk her life when she had children to think about.

She'd been so happy when she learned she was going to be a mother, but motherhood wasn't the life she had planned for herself. She hadn't planned for Elias to come in and change everything she knew about herself.

"How long do you want to wait before we try again?" he asked her.

He wanted to be a father. He wanted a big family. He treated her beautifully. There were times when he looked at her with such tenderness in his eyes that she would swear he was as in love with her as she was with him. But she could never be sure. Life would be unbearable without him, but spending a life with him and wondering if he would be happier somewhere else would be nearly as painful.

"I think we need to put off this discussion for now. We need to know where you are going to work first, and then we can worry about the house and everything else. I don't want to think about the future. I have a few more days in paradise with you, and that's all I want to think about right now."

"Okay." He kissed her lips softly. "That's more than okay."

# Chapter 14

They finally left Costa Rica. Left that little slice of paradise and returned to Hideaway Island, which to Elias had once been paradise for them, too. But returning felt much different. It was as if a little bit of the happiness drained out of them as soon as they stepped foot off the plane. It made sense for them to feel that way. They had a lot of painful memories here, business left unfinished.

Elias stood behind Cricket as she let them into the house that was not theirs, but hers. A gift from her father. The reason they had escaped to Costa Rica. Her mother had said that he had been a guest there, and walking back in, he didn't feel any more at home.

This place would never be his home unless he had some ownership of it.

"It feels empty, doesn't it?" she asked as she turned to him once they were in the living room. "It's odd that it feels empty. It was just the two of us before we left, and it will be just the two of us until…" She trailed off, the sadness seeping into her expression.

She said she wasn't ready to try again. She had taken precautions to ensure that there wouldn't be another accident, and he was fine with that. He enjoyed being with just her. In Costa Rica, he had never felt closer to anyone in his life. But he sensed that even though she said she wanted to wait, she didn't. Or it could be something else. Something she wasn't telling him. He had felt a little distance between them the last couple of days. It left a funny feeling in the pit of his stomach. But he forced down his worry. This was a tough time for them. Everything was so up in the air. They just needed time to figure things out.

Things would settle down between them. Elias took a step toward Cricket and smoothed his hands down her bare arms. "I know what you mean. After the way we left here, I'm surprised the locks on the doors weren't changed."

Cricket looked up into his eyes, the worry clear in her tone. "My mother hasn't tried to contact you? She hasn't offered you your job back?"

"I don't want my job back."

"Yes, you do," she said in a fierce whisper. "It's because of me you aren't going back."

"You influence a lot of my decisions, but you didn't make me quit. It was time for me to move on. It's best to keep my family and my career separate. It will make Thanksgivings that much easier."

"If you wanted it back, Elias, I would ask her for you. If you wanted me to, of course. I've never asked her for anything. She would do this for me. She would have to or I don't think I could ever look at her the same way."

"You're worried about me and my job, and I'm worried that I've ruined the relationship between you and your mother."

"You can't ruin what was barely there. It's never been easy between us."

"You should call her," he urged. "Just let her know that we're back and that you're feeling all right." This wasn't sitting well with him. To him, family was everything, and he couldn't imagine a world where he was estranged from his family.

"No. I left with you that day for a reason. I chose my husband over my mother, and she needs to understand that what I do with my life is my business. If she can't respect my choices, she can at least respect me enough to keep quiet about them."

"I know, baby. Your mother wants what's best for you. I just think she doesn't know how to convey that. But we can't go the rest of our lives not speaking to her."

"I'm done talking about this, Elias," she said forcefully enough that he took a small step away from her. "She's my mother, and I'll decide when and how we communicate again." She shook her head, the anger clearing out of her eyes. "I'm sorry. I shouldn't have snapped at you. I'm tired."

"Do you need me to get you anything? Are you hungry?"

She looked at him for a long moment. There was love in her eyes. It was clear as day, and yet he had never heard her say it. He had never said it, either. Something was stopping him, some invisible wall blocking their words.

She closed the distance between them and kissed his cheek. "You don't have to take care of me anymore, Elias. I'm going to go rest for a few hours."

She walked away, leaving him alone and feeling off center. He wanted to take care of her, not because she needed to be taken care of, but because she was his wife and he was in love with her.

The next afternoon Carlos, Ava and Ava's husband, Derek, showed up to welcome them back to the island. They all seemed happy to see their brother again, and Elias seemed glad to be back around his siblings, because he spoke to them for hours, about Costa Rica and their trip and his mother and aunts. Cricket was happy that Elias's family was so close. There was never any stilted conversation. There was never strain between them. They all seemed to support each other unwaveringly.

It shouldn't make Cricket sad that her husband had so much love in his life, but it did. Because even with her inherited fortune and all her education, she didn't have that. She could never have the big family and the overabundance of love.

She had excused herself to the kitchen under the pretense of getting snacks for everyone. She had been gone for over ten minutes now. Slowly chopping veggies for a platter. She had tried to keep up with the conversation as best as she could, but she still felt like an outsider with the Bradley clan, an interloper. Unlike Virginia or Derek, because they had married into the family in love. Cricket had married into the family because she had been pregnant by one of its members, but now that baby was gone and the only connection she had to them seemed to be temporary at best.

She was glad Virginia wasn't here with her baby girl, Bria. That would have made things worse. That would have made this evening even harder than it was. It had been almost two months since her loss. In Costa Rica, she'd been distracted by the lush surroundings, the new experiences, the constant lovemaking with her husband. But back here, she was reminded that her own family was splintered, that her grief was still there right under the surface, that the insecurities about her marriage were too strong to ignore. Elias didn't want to live in this house or on this island. He had a bigger life planned for himself than he was currently living. And she had a career that she was proud of, one that she had wanted to grow—before that fateful night that placed Elias onto her path.

"You need help in here?" Ava asked as she breezed into the kitchen. Cricket had been around Ava many times before, but she still couldn't get over how effortlessly beautiful she was.

"Did they send you to see what was taking me so long?" Cricket tried to inject some humor into her voice. "I need to have these vegetables cut into precisely two-inch pieces. Research says that's the right length for digestion."

"Is that true?" Ava raised one of her perfectly sculpted brows.

"Probably not," Cricket admitted. "I was thinking and kind of got lost in my thoughts."

"You want to talk? Not about your trip or the weather. I mean really, *really* talk."

"I'm fine."

"No, you're not. It's okay not to be, to tell someone that you aren't. There are certain things I can't speak to my husband about. I run to Virginia and spill my guts. Who do you go to when you need that?"

"I don't go to anyone. I don't have anyone like that in my life."

"I can be that person for you."

"But you're his twin. How do I know you two

don't have some sort of freaky twin connection going on? Your thoughts are probably linked."

"Trust me, they aren't. Thank God, because I'm pretty sure we'd both be in trouble if that were the case. Tell me what's going on inside that brainy head of yours."

"You know that the baby wasn't planned. It was something that just happened. And I was happy about it. I had all these plans that suddenly changed when I got pregnant. I was publishing my work. I was traveling the world conducting research. I was teaching at some of the most respected universities in the world. And then I put it all on hold for Elias, for the family I was going to have with him."

"And now that family is gone."

"And now I can't help but wonder if my mother was right. Maybe in its own terrible, tragic way, this was for the best. I lost some of myself in him. I think I might want it back."

Ava's expression was neutral for a moment, but then Cricket saw understanding in her eyes. "You're not sure if you're meant for the quiet life of dedicated wife and mother."

"I love him, Ava. Only God knows how much I do, but he wants a bunch of kids. He wants to be the kind of father you had. He wants to recreate his childhood with our children, but we aren't your parents. Elias is a surgeon, and I lived with a surgeon before. It's three-day shifts and twenty-hour surgeries. It's constant maneuvering to get to the top. And

I'll be alone again. But this time it will be worse, because I'll be alone with children who are barely going to know their father."

"I see your point." Ava nodded. "This is heavy. Have you talked to Elias about it?"

"What am I supposed to say? 'Give up your dream, the thing you've worked so hard to achieve so I won't be lonely'? 'Forget about all those lives you could have saved and stay home with me so we can watch TV together'? I can't say any of those things to him, because I know him too well. He would give them up to make me happy, because he thinks that's what a good husband should do, even if, in the long run, it makes him unhappy. I don't want him to be unhappy. I couldn't live with myself if he were."

"And he couldn't bear it if you were, either."

"What do you think I should do?"

"The thing that's the hardest to do. Compromise. It's the only way to make things work."


They had been back on Hideaway Island for over a week now. Cricket had been very quiet—most days she holed herself up in her office, claiming that she had to write. He knew that she had to write, that she had a book that was overdue, but part of Elias felt that Cricket was hiding herself from him. For some reason he'd thought that they would fall into some sort of routine when they got back, but there was no routine for them to fall into. Everything was so up in the air. Nothing had been settled. Not about her parents, or where they would live. They had no further discussions of their future. They were just drifting along.

Elias had gone back to picking up shifts at the local hospital and seeing patients as a primary care physician to pass the time. He was ready to go back to surgery. Physically. His hand had never felt better, but mentally...he wasn't sure yet. Maybe he was afraid he had lost his passion. Maybe he was afraid of being out of practice for so long, thought he would screw it up. Or maybe he just wasn't ready to leave his wife. They ate dinner together every night. They shared breakfast in the morning. There was nothing too important that happened in the small island hospital that he couldn't pick up the phone and call her when he wanted to.

But if he went back, followed the career path he'd always wanted, this simple, quiet life he had gotten used to would disappear. And yet he had already taken the first steps to being a surgeon again.

"You look very handsome in a suit. I haven't seen you in one since our wedding day," Cricket said to him as she smoothed her hand down his lapel.

"That was a good day." He leaned down to kiss her lips gently.

"Was it? I don't recall either of us being particularly happy."

"I was nervous and scared. I knew my life was about to change forever. How were you feeling?"

"Like you hated me."

"You know that's not true now, don't you?"

She hugged him tightly, resting her cheek against his chest. He felt the subtle sadness in her, and it worried him. "You're my all-time favorite husband."

"Have there been other husbands that I was unaware of?"

"You're the first, but I think I might be one of those women who would like to get married five or six times. Variety is the spice of life, you know. But I'll always have a soft spot for my first."

He grinned at her and smoothed his hand down her back. "Where will I be while you are marrying all these other men? Unless you plan on doing away with me."

"I don't know where you'll be." They had been joking, but there was a seriousness in her voice that he couldn't ignore.

"Are you sure you're okay with me going in to Miami for the meeting with Florida General?"

"You're better than Florida General. It's the worst hospital in the city. If you were hurt, I wouldn't want you to be treated there."

"But I could turn things around, or at least help to."

"You're talented and brilliant and sexy, and they would be lucky to have you. You'll be fine wherever you end up."

"Cricket, I…" He wanted to say that he loved her, but something stopped him. He hoped he had been reading too much into it, but the past couple of days, she'd been talking as if he had plans of going through this journey without her.

*Wherever* you *end up.* You *have to decide what* you *want.*

It was never *we*. It bothered him, and more than that, he worried about what she saw for their future.

"What is it?" She looked up at him.

"I'm not staying overnight in Miami. I'll be back on the last ferry."

"I'll pick you up."

"This is just a meeting. I don't even know if I want the job. I have a few options. I thought I would investigate this one in case you wanted to stay close to home."

"I want you to go where you'll be happy." She kissed his cheek. "Come on, let's get you to the ferry. You don't want to be late."

## Chapter 15

When Cricket arrived back at the house after dropping Elias off at the ferry, she noticed a familiar car parked in the driveway. She would recognize her mother's sleek black Aston Martin anywhere. Part of Cricket wanted to turn her car around and hide out in the ice cream parlor downtown for the next few hours, gorging herself on hot-fudge sundaes until she was sure her mother had left.

But she knew she couldn't do that. For all her mother's faults, she hadn't raised a woman who ran away from conflict. Cricket knew that this conversation had to happen. Realistically she knew she couldn't go on not speaking to her mother. Her family was so small. There was no way it could continue to be fractured.

Cricket got out of her car, but instead of walking inside her house, she walked around to the back and found her mother sitting on the sand just beyond the house. Her shoes were off, her toes buried in the cool sand. It wasn't a side of her mother that Cricket saw often. But she had seen it before. They used to vacation on this island. And there had been one glorious summer when Cricket had both of her parents there for an entire two months. Her mother had hurt her knee in an accident and couldn't work, and her father had decided to take off time to be with them. It was one of the few times in Cricket's life when she'd felt like she had a real family. A normal family that spent time together.

"I thought you said that one of the rudest things a person could do was drop by unexpectedly."

"That doesn't apply to mothers." Dr. Lundy looked up at her. "Mothers are allowed to say and do rude things to their daughters, and their daughters are just supposed to know that their mothers love them and respect them and don't mean to hurt them."

"Hmm." Cricket sat next to her mother. "Is that right?"

"Yes." She was quiet for a moment. "You're really in love with him, aren't you?"

"From the day I met him."

"And he's good to you, isn't he? He quit his job

at my hospital. I've heard he's been looking around the country. I've gotten calls about him already."

"He's a damn good doctor. I hope you recognize that. If he treats his patients anywhere near as good as he treats me, you shouldn't let him go."

"He's not playing hardball, is he? This isn't a ploy to force my hand."

"No, Mom. It's not about his job. It never was. The way you carry on about it makes me feel like you think that somebody like Elias couldn't possibly be in love with someone like me. That I'm so stupid, I would allow this man to get me pregnant and marry me in order to further his career. There are more important things than work. But it doesn't seem that way to you."

"Of course he could fall in love with you. You're beautiful and brilliant. I'm your mother. I don't think anyone is good enough to be with you. You have to admit that this situation was odd. He's my top doctor, whom I banned from my hospital for punching a patient's boyfriend, and then he shows up married to my only child. And you were pregnant. What would you have thought if you were me?"

"We really wanted that baby. Elias really wanted to be a father and—"

"I hurt you both deeply by diminishing your loss. But what I failed to make clear to you is that I have seen how deeply Elias loves you over the past few months. He worries about you. He takes care of you, and when you were in the hospital he was barking out orders like he was in charge of the world just to make sure you got what you needed. He's a good man and a good husband. I'm glad you married him. You can get pregnant again—right away, if you would like—your father and I would be overjoyed to have a grandchild. But now you have this time to spend together. Take advantage of it. Learn how to be together. I had five years with your father before we had you, and I think that time was good for us. We knew who we were and what we wanted out of life individually before we brought you into this world."

Her mother had just said something very deep to her. Cricket needed to know who she was and what she wanted from life, because she didn't think she could ever truly be a good wife to Elias if she didn't.

Elias had gotten out of bed very quietly that morning. He was off to the Midwest for another interview. This time it was a big one. A dream job at one of the best hospitals in the nation. For the past few weeks he had been traveling all over Florida, interviewing for jobs. He had been offered a few positions as head of a department at lower-ranking hospitals. They would keep him fairly close to his family, but he knew that with his long hours and being even farther away from Hideaway Island that he would rarely get to see them. He knew he wouldn't be happy at those places. And if he was going to be away from his family, he might as well be at a place he could be proud to work for, so he was taking this chance.

He had to be on the first ferry out that morning, so he had said goodbye to Cricket last night. They had made love for hours. He hadn't meant to. He had simply meant to kiss her, but that kiss had turned into more and he couldn't stop himself. He couldn't just take her once; he had to take her as many times as he could until they both passed out from exhaustion. He knew that he should have gone to sleep so he could be well rested for his journey, but he had needed her more than he needed the eight hours. The way she had clung to him afterward... It was as if she was telling him that she didn't want him to leave her.

But not once had she asked him not to go. She had been nothing but supportive these past few weeks. She left good-luck messages on his phone. Tucked notes into his suit pockets, encouraged him the way any good wife would. But there was something she wasn't telling him, something she was holding back. He had felt it ever since they got back from Costa Rica, but he couldn't put his finger on exactly what it was.

He walked back into their bedroom, fully dressed and ready to go. He just needed to kiss her one last time before he left. Even though he'd said goodbye to her last night, he couldn't leave without doing that. But instead of finding her curled up beneath the covers, he saw her sitting in her overstuffed armchair, looking out the window. She was wearing a simple sundress, her curls wild, her eyes still sleepy.

"What you are doing out of bed?"

"I thought you had gone already. I was waiting for my lover to come in and ravage me."

He grinned at her. "I still have time to murder a man before I leave."

"I'm taking you all the way to the airport. I booked passage for the car on the ferry. I'm going to be with you until security separates us."

"You don't have to do that. It's out of the way."

"It isn't. I'm planning to spend the day with my father. He's going to make me French toast and then take me to the toy store." She was quiet for a moment. "I need to take you to the airport, Elias. You'll be gone longer than overnight. This will be the longest we've been apart since we got married."

"It's only a couple of days."

"I'm going to have to get used to being alone once you go back to being a surgeon full-time."

"That's not true."

"But it is. I grew up with a surgeon. Your patients will have to come first. I know that. I'm prepared for it."

It would be just like before. Fifteen-hour surgeries. Exhaustion. Shifts that never seemed to end, but he had found huge satisfaction out of it. A huge sense of accomplishment. But now he had a wife whom he found more than satisfaction with, whom he found happiness with. Maybe going back and doing what he loved and being with the woman he loved at the same time would make him even happier, or maybe it would pull him in too many different directions.

In order to give his all to what mattered the most, something else he loved was going to have to suffer.

"Do you want me to stay home? I won't go to this interview. Just say the word and I'll stay."

"No. You're going to go. You're going to be offered this job."

"You don't know that."

"I do. I know my mother put in a good word for you. She's well respected across the country."

"You didn't ask her to do that, did you? I want to be hired on my own merits."

"I didn't have to ask her, and you should know my mother well enough by now to know that she won't do anything she doesn't believe is right. She has worked with you. She knows how good a surgeon you are. You deserve this job."

"I wish you would stop being the supportive wife and tell me what you want."

"That's easy. I want you to be happy. That's all I've ever wanted."

"Kiss me." He took a step toward her, and she put up her hand to stop him.

"I'll only kiss you when we are saying goodbye at the airport. You know what happens when we start kissing. I end up pregnant. You end up out of a job. You won't be blaming me for this one."

"Kissing you is what led me to marrying you."

"I know."

"I wouldn't take back that kiss, even if my life depended on it."

She looked at him for a long moment with so much emotion in her eyes, it nearly took his breath away. "I'm getting my keys and leaving this bedroom right now. Neither one of us will be safe if I don't."

She was right to go, because if he was with her any longer, he would miss his flight.

Cricket's father kissed her forehead the next morning. She had just planned to spend the day in Miami before she headed back to the island, but she couldn't force herself to leave the warmth of her parents' home. Her house would feel too empty without Elias. The sheets would smell of his skin. There would be little signs of him all over the place. She didn't want to face it. Having him and not being able to be with him was far worse than never having had him at all.

"Good morning, princess."

"Good morning, Daddy. How did you sleep last night?"

"Okay. I heard you wandering around last night."

"I'm sorry. I didn't mean to wake you."

"I wasn't awake because I heard you. I was awake because I was concerned about you."

"Why?" She looked up at her father, who clearly was worried. "I'm fine."

"Bug, I know you better than you know yourself."

"I got an email last night from a colleague I used to work with in Boston. He offered me a job. They are starting a new medical anthropology department at the university he heads. He wants me to run it. But the job is in London. I would head up a department in one of the most prestigious universities in the world."

"Tell me what you want to hear from me, and I'll say it."

She frowned in confusion. "Tell me what you think about it. I want you to be truthful."

"If you think I want my only child living on a different continent, you're insane. But I also recognize how big of an opportunity this is for you, and I will be excited for you. Still, this brings up a hundred more questions."

"Like how I can entertain a job offer when my husband is interviewing for his dream job in Wisconsin?"

"Yes, and more importantly, is this job in London that you weren't looking for one that you want to take?"

It was a good question, one that made her pause and think. "I don't want to be just the wife of a surgeon. I want to do more with my career. I want to leave a mark on this world, and for a moment that job offer seemed like an amazing thing, but then I got a text from Elias's sister. She was just checking in on me. She said she would come over if I wanted, because she knows I have a hard time going to sleep without him."

"She sounds like a wonderful person."

"His entire family is wonderful. I don't know how I would have gotten through these past few months without them, and it's made me realize that I don't want to leave Hideaway Island. I want to be close to my parents. I want to be surrounded by family. All the time."

"That's a beautiful thing, Cricket. You need to tell your husband that."

"I will. As soon as he calls me tonight."

## Chapter 16

Instead of calling Cricket, like he usually did when he was away on these trips, Elias pulled out his laptop and opened his video-chat app. He had never been this far away from her since they had gotten married. He had never gone so long without seeing her face, and while he had been busy, meeting with the heads of the hospital and touring the massive groundbreaking facility, he missed Cricket. He missed having dinner with her every night. He missed sharing coffee with her in the morning. And he was very aware that all that would change the moment he accepted a position as a surgeon again.

Cricket accepted the call, and seeing her pretty face put him at ease. She was in a pink nightie, her thin cotton bathrobe hanging loosely around her shoulders, and he could see just a hint of her skin, which was sweet and arousing at the same time.

"Hello, my husband."

"Hello, my wife. How are you today?"

"I'm okay. I stayed at my parents' house last night. When I came home, I had a long lunch with Virginia and Ava. We went shopping and then came back to the house and made cupcakes."

"You made cupcakes?" He grinned. Cricket had never baked. She had just started to cook a couple of months ago, out of necessity. She'd said that she needed to learn how to feed their child, but baking was something entirely different.

"Virginia said it was what girls do when they get together sometimes."

"Did you like it?"

"I loved it. I wish she had never shown me how to do it. I'm afraid I'll now have to eat cupcakes at least twice a week."

"I'll help you eat them."

"So tell me how everything went. I've been nervous for you."

"Everything went incredibly well. I thought Miami Mercy had state-of-the-art equipment, but you should see this place. They are on the cutting edge of medicine. The work they do here will change millions of lives. I was honored to even be considered and was blown away that they offered me a spot on their cardiothoracic team."

"You got the job! I knew you would get it." She smiled at him. "Are you okay with giving up trauma? I don't think you'll see much of it there."

"I wanted trauma for the excitement, but here I'll get to perform experimental procedures, try new techniques. I'll be learning from the best. That is, if you think I should take it."

"Of course I think you should take it! We've been through this before. This is an opportunity that you can't pass up. Take the job. I know you'll love it. When do you start?"

"That's the thing—they want me to start immediately. The surgeon I would be replacing is retiring, and he wants me to shadow him and get the lay of the land before he goes. They want me there tomorrow. They will pay for temporary housing and all our moving expenses. I just need you to overnight me some stuff. I was thinking that you could join me early next week."

The happy mask Cricket had been wearing slipped from her face, and the sadness that she had been hiding for the past few weeks was now evident. He had been waiting for it to appear. He knew in his gut that she hadn't been okay with any of this.

"I won't be joining you next week, Elias."

"Then when? The week after?"

"I don't know how long it will take. I've decided I don't want to leave Hideaway Island. I need to be near family. Yours and my own, and in Wisconsin, I know I won't be able to be happy."

"But you just told me to take the job. Do you want me to reject the offer?"

"No, I want you to take it. You have to take it. You'll live there, and I'll stay here. This job will be a huge part of your life, and I don't want you worrying about me or my happiness. I want you to stay there and do what you are meant to do. Do what you would be doing if we had never met and I had never gotten pregnant."

"What about us?"

"Maybe we need to be apart for a while. You need to adjust to your job, and I need to figure out what I'm going to do about my own. I've still got research that I want to conduct overseas. There are still things I want to accomplish, and this might be the perfect time."

What she was saying made sense. Logically he knew that if she wanted to go overseas, this would be the best time for her to do it. He was going to be incredibly busy, not just with surgery but with learning all the aspects of his new job. He wouldn't be able to be with her very often. Because he knew if he took the job here, his pride wouldn't allow him to give anything but his all. But he still felt crushed. Like somebody had squeezed him until every ounce of oxygen had left his body.

This felt like an ending. It *was* an ending, because they both knew they couldn't have a real marriage with both of them so far away and so focused on their careers.

"Is this what you really want, Cricket?" It wasn't what he wanted, but there was no compromising here. One of them would have to give up something major, and he wanted her to be happy.

Maybe being married to him didn't make her happy.

She opened her mouth to respond, but it seemed as if the words stuck in her throat. She said nothing, just nodded once, the tears welling in her eyes.

"This feels bad," he admitted. "A few months ago I was planning the rest of my life, and now we're talking about being apart."

"You wouldn't have married me if I wasn't pregnant. We both know that. I wasn't in your plans. Being a surgeon was in your plans."

How could he argue with that? He had never planned to get hurt, either, or to meet her, or to fall so damn hard in love, but it had happened and he didn't regret a moment of it. But clearly she did.

"I have to go, Elias." She swiped the tears from her face. "But I love you. I was in love with you the day I married you, and I don't think I'll ever be able to stop."

The screen went blank, and he jumped up from his chair. "What!" But she was gone, and soul-crushing devastation bloomed into something that felt a lot like hope.

He picked up his cell phone and dialed her number, but she didn't pick up. His next call was to a taxi.

Elias had called Cricket once. Just once. Then nothing all night. She hadn't picked up the phone the one time he called, because she couldn't listen to what he had to say. But his continued silence said far more than any words could. He was okay with them going their separate ways. And it confirmed what she had expected all along. She had interrupted his life. A wife was the last thing he had wanted. She had given him back his freedom. It was the logical thing to do. It was the right thing to do, but it was the hardest thing she'd ever had to do.

She'd tried not to cry last night, because crying wouldn't change a thing. She had fallen in love. It had been a beautiful few months. She couldn't regret it, because now she knew how well she should be treated. She knew what a truly good man was. She knew what passion and true lust were. She knew it was possible to feel deep, unending emotion for someone, and she'd learned that she was worthy of love. There was no way she could regret this marriage, but she could mourn it. Because she was fairly certain there wasn't another man on earth that she could love more than Elias.

She got out of bed and walked out to the beach to sit in the cool sand. It was early in the morning. There weren't signs of any people. It was peaceful. The sound of the waves gently lapping the shore soothed her. This place was so damned beautiful. She had traveled the world, but her soul kept pulling her back here. This was where she wanted to spend her life. This was home for her.

"You can't just tell a man that you're in love with him and then hang up before he responds."

She turned around to see Elias standing on the beach behind her. He looked rumpled and exhausted, but he was there—and her heart stopped beating. He was supposed to be over a thousand miles away in Wisconsin.

"What are you doing here? You're supposed to be accepting that job."

"I'm here to yell at you. Why the hell didn't you answer my call?" He walked closer to her. "I had to take four connecting flights and travel all night. I haven't had any sleep, and now I'm mad as hell."

"You only called once. I thought it was a mistake. You didn't even leave a message."

"Oh, so you did hear the phone? You just ignored it. And there I was wondering if you had gotten abducted by aliens or kidnapped. I was thinking the worst, and you just didn't want to pick up my call."

"I didn't want to hear what you had to say."

"Why not?"

"I didn't want to hear you let me down easy."

"Let you down easy? Let you down easy! You don't know me at all, do you?"

"I know that you have wanted to be a surgeon your entire life. That you went to medical school to be a doctor because your father couldn't follow his dreams. I know that you never planned to have a wife. I know if you'd had it your way, we never would have seen each other again."

"You're an idiot."

"You're an ass!"

"I'm an ass who's in love with you." He knelt down before her. "Can't you tell, Cricket? Can't you feel how much I love you?"

"I wish you'd told me that sooner. I thought you were just being nice."

"I'm not that nice! Nobody is that nice, Cricket. This is about you thinking you're not enough. But when the hell are you going to get it? When are you going to trust me enough to know that I'm not going to hurt you?"

"When you love somebody as much as I love you, it's scary. I keep thinking that this can't be real. That it's impossible for anything to be this good."

"I fell in love with you that first night we met. We were on the beach. It was twilight, and I couldn't stop looking at you. I only stayed away afterward because I didn't trust my feelings. I thought love at first sight was crap, but I loved you, and then you told me you were pregnant and I knew I had my shot to marry you without you thinking I was insane."

She frowned at him. "I *did* think you were insane."

"But you said yes when you didn't have to, and I asked you when I knew we could coparent without being a couple. I knew being with you was better than being without you. I want to be with you. I want to stay married to you for the rest of my life. I'm in love with you. What do I have to do to prove it to you?"

She had felt the same exact way. Never before had she experienced such a rush of feelings for anyone. She'd never thought that emotions like that were possible. At least not for her. And that's why she made no move to keep their connection going. She thought it was a fluke, and because of that she'd almost lost out on the love of her life. They had almost lost out on each other.

"You came home," she said as tears slipped down her face. "That's enough." She cupped his face and pressed her lips to his. "But what about your career? That's a job of a lifetime."

"You won't be happy there and I won't be happy without you, so it's not a question for me. I need to be where you are."

Cricket closed her eyes. "I feel so damn guilty. That's why I told you to stay! You weren't supposed to come rushing back here and make me love you more. I won't be able to forgive myself if I let you give up this job for me." She opened her eyes. "Call them and tell them there was an emergency here. I'll go back with you. We'll make it work—as long as we love each other, I know we can make things work."

He sat beside her in the cool sand and looked out at the ocean. "There's only one problem with that plan. I called them last night and turned down the position."

"Why did you do that? I could have wanted a divorce. You shouldn't have been so impulsive."

"You sound like your mother."

"You take that back!"

He chuckled and slipped his hand into hers. For somebody who had just thrown away his shot at a dream job, he was awfully relaxed. Happy, even. "I turned down that job because I have a shot at something I want more."

"You're going back to Miami Mercy? Did my mother tell you that she was going to make you the head of trauma?"

"No. I'm going to be working full-time at Hideaway Hospital. Instead of having the people here go off island for surgery, I'm going to operate here."

"Is that what you really want to do?"

"The job comes with amazing benefits."

"Does it?"

"I'll get to have coffee with my wife every morning. I'll get to eat dinner with her when I come home. I'll get to go to my children's soccer games. I get to have a life and be happy. I get to be with the woman I love as much as I possibly can."

"Those do sound like good benefits." She rested her head on his shoulder. "Remind me to send Giselle a thank-you card."

He looked over at her, surprised. "Why do you need to thank her?"

"Because if she wasn't who she was, then you never would have pretended to be my boyfriend and I would have never fallen in love with you that night."

"I think we need to send her more than a card. Maybe a bottle of wine and some flowers."

"And an invitation to our wedding."

"We had one of those already."

"I know, but I think I would like to have another ceremony. Right here on the island in front of our families."

"Nothing would make me happier than to marry you all over again."

\* \* \* \* \*

*Also check out these other sensual and emotional titles in Jamie Pope's*
TROPICAL DESTINY *series:*

*SURRENDER AT SUNSET*
*KISSED BY CHRISTMAS*
*MINE AT MIDNIGHT*

*Available now from Harlequin Kimani Romance!*

KIMANI™
ROMANCE

## COMING NEXT MONTH
### Available October 17, 2017

### #545 TAMING HER BILLIONAIRE
*Knights of Los Angeles* • by Yahrah St. John
Maximus Knight is used to getting what he wants, so seducing gallery owner
Tahlia Armstrong into turning over her shares of his family's company should
be easy. But when a shocking power play threatens their passionate bond,
Tahlia must decide if she can trust Max with her heart.

### #546 A TOUCH OF LOVE
*The Grays of Los Angeles* • by Sheryl Lister
After an explosion shattered Khalil Gray's world, café owner Lexia Daniels
becomes the only person he can't push away. The ex-model is happy to explore
their chemistry as long as it means resisting real emotion. But playing by his
old rules could cost him the love he never thought he'd find...

### #547 DECADENT DESIRE
*The Drakes of California* • by Zuri Day
Life's perfect—except for the miles that separate
psychologist Julian Drake from his longtime love,
Nicki Long. So when the Broadway dancer returns
to their idyllic town, Julian is beyond thrilled. But
Nicki's up against a deadly adversary that could end
her future with the Drake of her dreams...

### #548 A TIARA UNDER THE TREE
*Once Upon a Tiara* • by Carolyn Hector
Former beauty queen Waverly Leverve can barely
show her face in public after an embarrassing meme
goes viral. But business mogul Dominic Crowne
wants to sponsor Waverly in a pageant scheduled
for Christmas Eve. Can he help her achieve
professional redemption and find his Princess
Charming under the mistletoe?

# Get 2 Free Books,
## Plus 2 Free Gifts —
### just for trying the
## Reader Service!

# *LOVE*
# Harlequin
# romance?

Join our Harlequin community to share your thoughts and connect with other romance readers!

Be the first to find out about promotions, news, and exclusive content!

Sign up for the Harlequin e-newsletter and download a free book from any series at

## www.TryHarlequin.com

---

**CONNECT WITH US AT:**

Harlequin.com/Community

 Facebook.com/HarlequinBooks

 Twitter.com/HarlequinBooks

 Instagram.com/HarlequinBooks

 Pinterest.com/HarlequinBooks

ReaderService.com

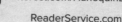

**ROMANCE WHEN
YOU NEED IT**

Want to give in to temptation with
steamy tales of irresistible desire?

Check out **Harlequin® Presents®,
Harlequin® Desire** and
**Harlequin® Kimani™ Romance** books!

**New books available every month!**

---

**CONNECT WITH US AT:**

Harlequin.com/Community

 Facebook.com/HarlequinBooks

 Twitter.com/HarlequinBooks

Instagram.com/HarlequinBooks

Pinterest.com/HarlequinBooks

ReaderService.com

**ROMANCE WHEN
YOU NEED IT**

PGENRE2017

Need an adrenaline rush from nail-biting tale
(and irresistible males)?

Check out **Harlequin® Intrigue®**
and **Harlequin® Romantic Suspense** books!

# New books available every month!

---

# Reward the book lover in you!

Earn points from all your Harlequin book purchases from wherever you shop.

Turn your points into *FREE BOOKS* of your choice
OR
*EXCLUSIVE GIFTS* from your favorite authors or series.

Join for FREE today at
**www.HarlequinMyRewards.com.**

Harlequin My Rewards is a free program (no fees) without any commitments or obligations.

MYR17

# Love Inspired®

## Inspirational Romance to Warm Your Heart and Soul

---

Join our social communities to connect with other readers who share your love!

Sign up for the Love Inspired newsletter at **www.LoveInspired.com** to be the first to find out about upcoming titles, special promotions and exclusive content.

---

### CONNECT WITH US AT:

Harlequin.com/Community

 Facebook.com/LoveInspiredBooks

 Twitter.com/LoveInspiredBks